JESSICA BECK

THE DONUT MYSTERIES, BOOK 37

APPLE-STUFFED
ALIBIS

The First Time Ever Published!

The 37th Donut Mystery.

Jessica Beck is the *New York Times* Bestselling Author of the Donut Mysteries, the Classic Diner Mysteries, the Ghost Cat Cozy Mysteries, and the Cast Iron Cooking Mysteries.

For absent friends,
Gone, but not forgotten.

When a prominent member of the community is murdered, the list of suspects is longer than the lines during a free donut giveaway. Odd couple Suzanne and her stepfather, Phillip, dig into the case together to unmask the killer, and in the course of their investigation, the two amateur sleuths become embroiled in some of the worst aspects of small-town life as they struggle to find the murderer.

CHAPTER 1

M Y PLAN WAS TO PRESENT the event to the community as a celebration of my anniversary of owning Donut Hearts—the shop I ran in our quaint little town of April Springs, North Carolina—but what most folks didn't realize was that there was another, and for me, much more upsetting, purpose to the event as well. The plain truth was that my business was in trouble, potentially serious financial distress, and if I didn't come up with a way to pull it out of the slump it was currently in, I might not own the place much longer.

The last thing I needed to deal with was murder, but unfortunately, that was exactly what happened, and in the end, I nearly lost everything I held near and dear, including my own life.

"There's no doubt about it. I'm in serious trouble," I told Jake as I looked at him with a frown from across the kitchen table after I'd gotten home as soon as I'd closed Donut Hearts for the day.

"Just how bad is it?" he asked me as he closed the book he'd been reading and gave me his full attention.

"If things don't turn around, and I mean fast, we're going to have to do some serious cutting back here *and* at the donut shop, and what's worse, it *still* might not be enough. I may have to lay Emma and Sharon off and run the entire place seven days a week by myself, and even *that* might not be enough to keep me afloat until cool weather comes back." It was currently the dead of summer, always the slowest time of the year for us at Donut Hearts, the business I'd bought after my divorce from my first husband and had run ever since, but this had been the worst slump I'd ever seen in my life, at least as far as the business was concerned.

"I have three suggestions," Jake said as he studied me closely after pondering the situation for a few minutes, "and I can tell you up front that you aren't going to like *any* of them."

"As much as I appreciate the offer, you're not coming to work for me at the donut shop." I loved my husband dearly, but I knew that having him around twenty-four-seven was more than either one of us could take. I didn't know how retired married couples managed it. Even Momma and Phillip, one of the happiest married couples I knew, spent quite a bit of time apart during the day, Momma with her various business interests and Phillip with his cold police cases he loved to investigate.

"Believe it or not, that thought never even crossed my mind," he said, looking suitably horrified by the mere suggestion of it.

"And I won't take out a mortgage on the shop," I said, cutting him off from another avenue I refused to go down. It had long been a point of pride for me that I owned the donut shop free and clear, and the idea of the bank possessing any part of it simply was not an option. I'd bought the place with just about every last dime of my divorce settlement from Max, the Great Impersonator, and it represented my freedom from a destructive and oppressive relationship and a new lease on life that was all mine and just mine.

"I'm not silly enough to suggest that, or even that we take out a mortgage on the cottage," Jake said, looking around at our home.

It was a good thing, too. Momma had given us the place when we'd gotten married, and it had been in family hands for generations. I wouldn't have parted with one square inch of it willingly, or even under gunpoint if it came down to that. "Well, other than those things, I'm willing to consider any options you might be able to suggest."

"Ask your mother for a short-term loan, at least until you can get back on your feet," Jake said, ticking one finger off his hand.

On the surface, it appeared to be a perfectly reasonable option. After all, my mother was quite wealthy in her own right, and I knew that it would give her great pleasure being able to help me out. The only problem was that I just couldn't bring myself to do it, since my stubborn streak was matched only by my mother's inclination to dig in her heels at the slightest provocation. I would have rather gone to the bank than to her for a loan, and Jake already knew how I felt about that. "No thanks," I said. "What else do you have?"

He grinned at me before he answered. "Well, at least you gave it some serious thought."

"I did," I said in protest.

"I wasn't being sarcastic. I was expecting an automatic rejection within a split second of offering it, but you waited at least three heartbeats before you turned it down."

"It's not that I have too much pride," I started to protest, but then I stopped. "That's not really true, is it? Maybe I have entirely too much of it, but owing her would be worse than having a mortgage with the bank."

"She might make it an outright gift," Jake offered.

It was most likely true, but that didn't change anything. "In a great many ways, that would just make it worse," I said.

"I know. On to number two, then. I've got a pension we can tap. I worked for the state police long enough to amass a tidy little sum, so why don't we use some of that now when we need it?"

"I can't do that, either," I said, though I answered more slowly still.

3

"Why not?" Jake asked as he started to cloud up. "You're always saying that we're a team. Why shouldn't we use that reserve? After all, it's *our* money, not just *mine*."

I had to be very careful how I answered him. I wasn't the only one in our marriage with more than their normal share of pride. "I suppose we could, but given the penalties we'd have to pay for withdrawing it early, it might not be worth the effort."

Jake looked surprised by my admission. "You've actually thought about it before?"

I had, but not in the way he thought. I knew when I brought the topic up with my husband, he'd offer his retirement account without blinking. I just couldn't bring myself to take it, not unless things got to be *much* worse than they were. I would have probably asked Momma for money before I took the pension funds from Jake, but he didn't have to know that. "I considered it," I admitted. "Is that good enough?"

"It's more than good enough," he said, smiling slightly. "Would you like to hear my last idea?"

"Why not?" I asked, leaning back in my chair to hear what he had to say.

"I could get a job," he said after a moment's pause. "Not full time and not permanent, but an old buddy from the state police is looking for help doing security for some bigwig CEO in Richmond, and he's willing to pay handsomely. The job should last only two weeks, and it starts this evening. The truth is that we both know that I've been itching to do something, anyway. I hate leaving you here all by yourself, but it could really help out with our financial crunch."

"Our need for the money aside, is this something that you *want* to do?" I asked him.

"Yeah, I think I do," he replied.

"Is it dangerous?" I asked.

"Suzanne, getting out of the bathtub is dangerous." It was

a standard answer for him, one that casually dismissed the possibility of mayhem.

"You take showers, though, so that's not a problem. Jake, you know what I mean," I said sternly. "Tell me the truth."

"There have been a few threats against the man, but Jim sincerely believes that it's the work of some nut sitting in his basement in his underwear writing threatening emails to folks he doesn't even know. He doesn't think we'll see the guy, let alone have to stop anything, but this lunatic has got the CEO spooked."

"Your friend could be wrong, though," I said, realizing that my husband was probably downplaying the danger for my sake. He'd dealt with more than his share of really bad people in the past, and I didn't like the idea of him putting himself in jeopardy again, especially for my sake.

"Suzanne, the truth is that it will be good for me, and if it will help keep Donut Hearts afloat until you can turn things around, where's the harm? It's a sacrifice for the two of us being apart, but we can handle it. What should I tell Jim? He needs an answer by two, and if I'm going, I need to leave as soon as possible."

It was now one thirty-two. "Jake Bishop, did you wait until the last possible second to ask me?" I queried with a grin.

"Hey, by my reckoning, I've got twenty-eight minutes left on the clock," he said, "but I knew you were doing the books after work today, and after hearing you complain about how slow business has been lately, I thought it might be prudent to hold off until I spoke with you." He was openly grinning now. "So what do you say?"

"That depends. I have one more question for you. Are your bags already packed?" I asked him as I returned his smile.

"I figured it wouldn't hurt, just in case you said yes," he

admitted sheepishly. "I can always unpack if you're dead set against me going."

I couldn't say no to this man or disappoint him if I could help it. I had a hunch that our money woes were just one more excuse to let him go, but the main reason was simply because he seemed excited about the prospect, something I hadn't seen in quite a while, so how could I say no to that? "Go, you big goof. Just promise me that you'll be careful."

"You bet," he said as he jumped up and kissed me soundly. "Oh, there's one other thing. Our employer has a thing about his people using cell phones on the job, so I may have trouble checking in with you on any kind of regular basis. Is that okay?"

"Don't worry about me. If I get in trouble here, I've got a dozen folks I can call on for help," I said, not realizing just how prescient I was being at the time.

"Excellent." He bolted for the bedroom and came out almost immediately again with a travel bag. Putting it down by the door, Jake swept me up in his embrace the moment I stood, and after lingering in his arms for a few moments longer than I probably should have, I pulled away. "Go on, then. Have fun."

"It's a serious job, you know," he reminded me, clearly trying to keep the grin off his face. "But thanks. I will. I love you."

"I love you, too," I said, and then he was gone.

I sat there for a few seconds feeling sorry for myself. The cottage had never felt emptier, and I knew what I had to do. I needed to go someplace else, somewhere I was almost always welcome, and the beauty of it was that I could get there on foot.

I grabbed my front-door key, and after locking the door behind me, I walked less than a hundred yards to my best friend's house.

If anyone could cheer me up, it would be Grace Gauge.

CHAPTER 2

"WHY SO GLOOMY, GUS?" GRACE asked me the moment she opened the door.

"Is it that obvious?" I asked her as I stepped inside her home. We'd grown up together, best friends for life. Having her still living just steps away, each of us in the houses we'd grown up in, was a bonus I was thankful for every day. Momma could read me better, but no one else in the world could, including Jake. It was only natural, I supposed. After all, Grace and I had a much longer history together.

"Not to the average person, but as we both know, I'm *anything* but average," she said with a grin. "Let me get us a pair of sweet teas and you can tell me all about it."

"Did you make the tea yourself?" I asked her as she headed for the kitchen. Grace was many things, but being skilled in any of the culinary arts wasn't one of them. On the surface of it, making sweet tea didn't seem that complicated, but in the South, it was a true art form. The drink had to be sweet enough to satisfy the most discerning palates but not enough to make your back teeth ache. The brand, the amount of time the tea steeped, the exact amount of sugar added, and a few other variables were all closely guarded secrets in most of the families I knew, and the debate between using regular tap water, spring water, well water, or bottled water was just one of the many debates that surrounded the preferred drink of the South.

"Don't worry, I bought a gallon from Trish at the diner," she said. "Why? Don't you think I'm capable of making good tea myself?"

"Capable? Of course you are. Whether you choose to is another question altogether," I said as I took a glass from her with a smile.

Grace tried to look stern, but she could only hold it for a second or two. As she began to laugh, I joined her, and I knew that I'd made the right decision coming to her. My best friend was usually good for whatever ailed me.

After we were seated in the living room, Grace said, "Tell me what's going on."

I brought her up to speed on everything, revealing more than I would have even to my own mother. When she heard that Jake had taken a job out of town, she frowned. "It must be serious for him to leave you."

"He's just going to be gone a few weeks," I protested. "It's not like he isn't coming back."

"I know that, you nit," she said. "Still, is his pay going to be enough to see you through?"

"Probably not," I told her. "It will help, but if things keep going the way they are, it's not going to be enough." I took a breath, and then I quickly added, "Let's get one thing out in the open. Don't you dare volunteer to offer me any money."

She grinned at me. "The truth is that thought never crossed my mind."

I frowned at her. "And may I ask why not? I thought we were friends."

Grace's smile intensified. "Suzanne, what would you do if I offered you a loan, or even an outright gift? You don't need to answer. You'd turn it down before I finished making my suggestion. So why waste our breath even discussing it?"

"That's a fair point," I said. "I'm open to other suggestions, though."

"When did you buy the shop? It was around this time of year, wasn't it?"

I hadn't even thought about it, but she was right. "As a matter of fact, I believe that my anniversary is in three days," I said.

"There's your answer. Throw a blowout celebration! Remind folks that you're here and that you've been serving them loyally for all of these years. If you do it right, you might just be able to turn things around yourself."

"Why didn't I think of that?" I asked her, amazed that the anniversary of me owning Donut Hearts had somehow slipped my mind.

"That's why I make the big bucks," she said with a smile. "Sometimes it just takes someone with a fresh perspective to point the way. Tell you what. I've got some vacation I have to use or lose, and I can't think of anyplace I'd rather be than here hanging out with you. I'll help."

"You could always take a trip with your boyfriend," I suggested.

"I suggested it, but the police chief said that he couldn't get away. I'm not so sure we're going to make it, Suzanne," she said with sorrow thick in her voice.

"I'm so sorry," I said. I knew the two of them had their share of problems, but I hadn't realized it was that serious. "Is there anything I can do?"

"I wish there was, but the man's married to his job, and I'm getting a little tired of just being his mistress." Grace shook her head for a brief moment. "Your party sounds exactly like what I need, too. Would you mind if I helped you plan it?"

"Are you kidding me? I'd love it," I said, making a mental note to say something to the chief. We'd been friends for years, and I was going to take advantage of it and upbraid him for his behavior with Grace. He could search for a hundred years and not find a better woman. Stephen Grant had no idea what was in store for him. "When can you get started?"

"How about right now?" Grace asked me with a smile. "This sounds like fun."

"Don't forget, we have a very serious goal in mind here," I reminded her.

"Sure, but we're not telling anyone else that. As far as April Springs is concerned, Donut Hearts is going to have a party, and the whole town is going to be invited!"

CHAPTER 3

"WHAT'S THIS?" I ASKED GRACE forty-five minutes later as she handed a printout to me. She'd been playing on her computer in her office while I'd been toying with ideas for a new donut in honor of the event in the living room. I hadn't been using a computer, though. A legal pad and a pen had been all that I'd needed. So far, I was leaning toward an apple-cherry cake donut, but a banana pudding–filled donut was also a real possibility, mainly because my husband adored the dessert treat, and I knew he'd love them, even if he wasn't home to taste one right away.

"I just ordered a giant donut for our party," she said with a grin. "It can fit on the roof, right?"

I studied the image of the giant donut—chocolate iced cake with ribbons of white icing and sprinkles—and I had to laugh. When Grace committed to something, she did it wholeheartedly. The price made me blanch a bit, though. After all, I was trying to make money, not lose it. "It's kind of expensive," I said before adding, "not that I don't love it."

"Relax, Suzanne. This is my treat. I think it's going to look fantastic on top of the shop."

"We'll have to get someone to make sure the roof can handle it. I thought it would be inflatable when I first saw it, but evidently it's made of fiberglass."

"That's probably not much heavier than regular plastic, is it, and how heavy could that be?" She held up an empty water bottle and shook it in the air. "This thing weighs next to nothing."

"True, but I'm not sure we're comparing apples to apples here. That donut is six feet across, and unless I'm mistaken, fiberglass weighs a lot more than plastic does. They make boat hulls out of the stuff, don't they?"

She frowned a bit. "Sorry. I'll see if I can cancel the rental."

I wanted to stop her, but I was afraid that it might be a problem, so I let her go ahead and make the call. After a very brief conversation, she hung up. "Okay, they won't refund my deposit. They claim they already left with it, so you'll probably see it in a few hours. Some people will do anything to make a sale. Maybe we could just prop it up *beside* the building when it gets here."

"No worries, Grace. I'll get a customer of mine to check it out this evening," I said. A new handywoman had moved to April Springs not that long ago. I missed Timothy, my old friend who had always tackled things like this for me not all that long ago. When he'd been murdered, no one had been able to step up and take his place. A few others had come and gone since, but this new woman seemed promising. Her van had a large sign on the side of it, Fix It Francie, with a cartoon of a woman in a tool belt brandishing a hammer in one hand and a handsaw in the other. Francie was overly fond of donuts, even though she probably didn't weigh much over a hundred pounds.

"Francie Mulligan?" Grace asked me.

"You've met?"

"She's done a few jobs around here for me. She's good."

"Her mother was a handywoman too, and she started taking Francie on her work calls with her as soon as she could walk," I said, relaying the story Francie had told me when we'd first met.

"I'll give her a call," Grace offered.

"I can do it right now myself," I said.

"Nonsense. I ordered the supersized donut, and installation

is included with the gift. If she's not free, we'll get someone else to do it." She glanced down at my notes. "Have you come up with a signature donut yet?"

"It's down to two," I said, explaining my preliminary ideas. One look at Grace told me she wasn't exactly overwhelmed with my ideas. "I'm open to suggestions, though."

"I just assumed that you'd make little birthday cake donuts, but your ideas are good, too."

I ripped off the top page and started sketching on the next clean sheet. "I see where you're going with the idea. We can make a simple white cake donut, add colored icing and sprinkles, and each donut can have one of those little candles on it, too. I love it! That's a great idea! Grace, you're an absolute genius."

"I just lit the match. You're the one who set the fire," she said.

"I'm not sure I'm thrilled with the analogy, but sure, why not? I need to lay in some extra supplies for the party. We can drive over to Union Square to Cheap Cheeps and buy a bunch of streamers and banners that all say Happy Birthday on them." Cheap Cheeps was a relatively new discount store that specialized in items for sale that no one else seemed to be able to sell. It had a stock of misprinted books, misaligned print jobs, discontinued lines, poorly researched products, and a host of other things, all offered at bare-bones pricing.

"Let's go," Grace said as she grabbed her purse.

"Right now?" I asked.

"As you pointed out earlier, we don't have a great deal of time. When we get an idea, we have to move on it."

"You're right," I said as I stood. "There's no time like the present."

"There it is," Grace said as she pointed to a building in Union Square that had been repurposed half a dozen times since the original tenant had moved out. A giant yellow duck on top of the roof moved in the wind, and someone had clearly painted the dozen straps holding it down the same canary yellow so they would blend in with the duck's body. It looked like a yellow bath toy on steroids, only one of the eyes was cocked a little to the side, giving the duck a distinct cross-eyed, quizzical expression.

"Is it just me, or is that duck a little off?" I asked Grace as she pulled into the parking lot, which was surprisingly crowded. "Where did all of these people come from?"

"Everybody loves a bargain," Grace said, "and as to your first question, everything *about* this place is a little off. Do ducks really go cheep?"

"I thought they quacked," I admitted as we approached the front door.

"So why didn't they call it Quack Cheap? Forget it, consider the question asked and answered. I don't think the semantics really have to add up. Let's grab a cart and see if we can find anything and everything that's donut themed."

"An anniversary motif would work, too," I said. "Or even a birthday banner or two."

Grace laughed as she started to pilot an oversized shopping buggy through the narrow aisles. "I'm not sure this store is sophisticated enough to have specific themes."

"Maybe not. All we can do is look."

After walking the aisles for twenty minutes, I was ready to give up. "All we found was an inflatable donut raft, and you've already got that covered. The anniversary stuff was pretty useless, too."

"The birthday section had a lot of choices," she said.

"I suppose. The graduation party area was stocked, too, but that doesn't mean we can use it, either." The party idea, as good as it had seemed at first, was beginning to feel a bit like a bust.

"Suzanne, we can't give up now," Grace said.

"Why not? Oh, that's right. The giant fiberglass donut deposit is nonrefundable." I stared at her for a second, she looked right back at me, and finally we couldn't contain it anymore. Grace and I started laughing out loud like a pair of lunatics. Folks around us were steering clear of us altogether, which made the situation even funnier. After I caught my breath again, I asked, "So, what should we do? Is our third choice going to be good enough?"

"Absolutely. We have birthday things. You've already sketched out some really cool birthday donuts, so let's go all in and make it a birthday party for the donut shop," she said.

"Between the two of us, we can make it work," I replied as we headed back to the birthday section. We went through the balloons, streamers, banners, hats, plates, and everything else birthday themed and started loading up. Our buggy was close to bulging, though our budget, as limited as it was, wasn't going to take much of a hit. Did it really matter that the B in birthday on some of the things had been printed backwards? Or that the flames for the candles on the banners didn't quite match up with their wicks? They were big, loud, and colorful, an easy way to attract attention, and of course, they were all indeed cheap, just as promised.

"This is going to be perfect," Grace said as she lingered at a pile of books marked down to twenty-five cents apiece. "Why are these so cheap?"

I picked one up and riffled through it. "Half the pages are upside down, and some of them are repeats. What good are they?"

"You'd think you were insane if you tried to actually read one of them," Grace answered.

"And yet they've clearly sold some copies," I said as I studied the display.

"You think that's bad, look at these," Grace said. She picked up a pack of plastic cups that looked perfectly fine at first glance, but after a closer examination, it was clear that the bottoms were missing out of each and every cup.

"That takes the dribble glass to an entirely new level."

"Maybe so, but they're awfully cheap." As she said it, a woman pushed past us and loaded some of the very cups we'd just been mocking into her cart. She was dressed in nice clothes, and she had an elegant look about her that didn't quite belong in the discount store. I glanced into her buggy and saw the oddest assortment of cast-offs, and of course, I couldn't seem to keep my mouth shut, which was a familiar problem for me. "Excuse me, but you do realize those don't have bottoms, right?"

"Aren't they cool?" the woman asked with more enthusiasm than anyone should have been showing over her purchases.

"But what good are the things you are buying?"

Her grin didn't diminish in the slightest. "I call this place my Imagination Station for shopping. All it takes is some thinking outside the box."

"For instance?" I asked, intrigued by this woman's spirit. "What possible use is a cup with no bottom?"

"I use them in my garden for new seedlings. I just put a cup around the new plant until it's too tough for the rabbits to eat. They work wonderfully."

"And these forks with two-inch handles?" I asked, digging into her buggy without invitation.

"I use those in the garden, too. I plant them with tines up to discourage critters from eating my crops. It works like a charm. Well, mostly," she said with a shrug. "Not everything pans out, but hey, I haven't really lost that much trying, have I?"

"Do you use *everything* in the garden?" Grace asked, clearly as intrigued as I was.

"Oh, no." She grabbed a small box and held it aloft. "These

aren't great as crayons, but they work beautifully as emergency candles. They're impossibly brittle to sharpen, but they stay lit for a long time. The list is endless. All it takes is a little creativity and an active imagination." She glanced into our cart. "Should I wish you a happy birthday?"

"It's for the anniversary of me buying my donut shop," I said.

The woman grinned at me. "But the anniversary pickings are sparse, aren't they? See, you're more like me than you realized." She seemed to be distracted by a teenaged employee stacking a new display. "Hey, is that industrial-sized nail polish he's putting up over there? I've got a zillion uses for that stuff. Happy hunting, ladies."

After she was gone, Grace turned to me. "When I grow up, I want to be more like she is."

"Don't we all," I said as I pointed our buggy toward the register. Just then I noticed a familiar face, one I knew well from April Springs. "Hey, isn't that Marybeth Jenkins over there?" Marybeth was the head of our local board of elections, a stylish, thin woman with lustrous black hair and the palest complexion I'd ever seen. She'd been the one who'd announced George Morris's shocking write-in mayoral victory long ago. The two of them had formed a bond working together in city hall over recent years, and at times we'd all wondered if their relationship had been something *more* than professional at any point along the way, but any attempts they may have made at getting together had ultimately been dashed by Cassandra Lane's arrival into the mayor's life. Once Cassandra had come into the picture, all other contenders for the mayor's heart went by the wayside. "Hey, Marybeth," I said as I approached her. She'd clearly been lost in thought looking at old Valentine's Day decorations, and unless I was mistaken, she'd been softly crying when I'd disturbed her. I touched her arm lightly. "Marybeth, are you okay?"

"Me? I'm fine," she said as she wiped away the tears and tried to smile. "It's these darned allergies. They hit me at the oddest times."

From the wistful look in her eyes, I doubted that pollen had generated her tears, but I wasn't going to say anything.

Grace didn't seem to feel that way, though. "Is it the mayor again?" she asked, much to my surprise. My best friend could be blunt to the point of brutality at times, but she meant well, and oftentimes she got to the root of problems much faster than I could ever manage to.

"What about him?" she asked, looking immediately defensive. Marybeth actually recoiled a bit from the question, stepping back and nearly knocking over a stack of what had to be boxes of really stale Christmas candy.

"Come on, Marybeth. Don't forget who you're talking to here," Grace said.

I shook my head, trying to warn Grace off the topic, but it had no impact whatsoever.

"I'm sure I don't know what you're implying," she said stiffly, and then she headed for the door, abandoning a nearly full buggy in the process.

"Marybeth, aren't you forgetting something?" I called out.

"I'll do my shopping later. Right now I've got to go," she said, not even glancing back at us as she hurried away.

"Was it something I said?" Grace asked after she was gone.

"You're not seriously asking me that, are you?" There was no way my best friend could be that thick. I knew her too well. "Your question about the mayor clearly rocked her back on her heels."

"Don't you think I know that? Suzanne, she needed a cold bucket of water on her head, and I decided it was high time that

I provided it. If she wants George so badly, she needs to go after him and stop pining away like some simpering little schoolgirl."

"That's kind of harsh, isn't it?" I asked her.

"It's exactly what she needs. You should hear the way she idolizes the man!"

"She's never said anything about George to me," I said.

"Marybeth and I have become quite a bit closer lately," Grace confessed, as though she were apologizing to me. "She came to me for advice on her makeup, and while we were chatting, it quickly became clear that she was in love with our dear mayor and has been for years."

"When did all of this happen?" I asked. I wasn't jealous of Grace having another friend. It just surprised me that this was the first I was hearing about it.

"We were at the grocery store a month ago as they were closing, and we started chatting in the checkout line. It was nearly nine o'clock," she added almost apologetically.

That hour was well past my bedtime, since I had to be at the donut shop by three a.m. most days. I usually awoke a little before that, which meant that if I was going to get even a modest amount of sleep, I had to go to bed pretty early. Of course Grace could and should have a life of her own after I was asleep.

"It's too bad she waited so long to make her move," I said. "The mayor is pretty well hooked these days."

"I wouldn't be so sure of that," Grace said a little cryptically.

I looked at her a moment before I spoke. "Why do you think that? Grace, what's going on? Have you heard something?"

"Just that Cassandra is putting a lot of pressure on George to run for higher office, and it's causing a great deal of tension between them."

This was the first I'd heard of it, but contrary to popular belief, Donut Hearts was not the hub for all gossip in April Springs. "Does she want him to run for state legislature?" I asked her. At first I thought it was an absurd idea, but then again, George had become rather deft at politics since he'd taken over as our mayor. Maybe it wasn't entirely out of the question after all.

"No, it's bigger than that. She wants him to run for governor," Grace said.

"Of *North Carolina*?" I asked, a pretty ridiculous concept taken at face value.

"Yes, of North Carolina. Evidently they've been arguing about it quite a bit lately. I'm not so sure that Marybeth doesn't have a chance if she just says something to the man about how she feels."

"Wow, I'm absolutely speechless," I said.

"I doubt it, but if it's true, it's got to be a first." Grace looked into our buggy. "Do we have enough for the celebration, do you think?"

"Coupled with your giant donut, we should be fine," I said, still reeling a little over trouble in paradise. "Let's check out and head back."

Grace looked at her watch. "Is there any chance we could grab an early dinner before we head back to April Springs? We're so close to Napoli's we could practically walk from here. You know that Angelica would be hurt if we were this close and we didn't at least come by and say hello."

Angelica DeAngelis and her beautiful daughters ran the best Italian restaurant in four counties, and besides that, she was one of my dearest friends. "Well, I wouldn't want anyone to think I was rude," I said with a grin. "Sure, why not?" The truth was that since Jake was gone, I had no real desire to dine alone. Having Grace eat with me at Napoli's wasn't a substitute for being with my husband, but it was a close second. As I paid for the party goods, I couldn't help wondering what the mayor had gotten himself into. We'd become friends a long time ago, and I hated the fact that he was having problems with his girlfriend, but when all was said and done, he was a grown man, and he'd have to figure out a way to deal with them himself.

I had enough problems of my own without having to worry about taking on any of his.

After all, I had a donut shop to save, and even if it took every last ounce of my energy, I was going to figure out some way to make it happen.

CHAPTER 4

"ANGELICA, IT'S SO GOOD TO see you," I said as I hugged the beautiful owner of Napoli's moments after walking into the restaurant. Not only was it my favorite place to eat out, but it also happened to be run by one of my best friends and her lovely daughters.

"Suzanne! Grace! I am doubly blessed today. What brings you here? Is there another murder case afoot? The police should hire the two of you, you are such good detectives."

Angelica was many things, but soft-spoken was not one of them. Several folks waiting for tables were watching us avidly, but since we weren't working on a case, I didn't really mind being overheard.

"We are here for your wonderful food. Isn't that enough of a reason?" I asked her with a smile. "Wow, you're really crowded for it being so early."

"Sophia has been running more specials to keep us busy during our off hours," she said as she grabbed a pair of menus. "Follow me."

"You've got to be kidding me! We were plainly here first," a stuffy man in a suit said angrily as Angelica started to lead us into the dining room.

She stopped in her tracks, turned to him, and stared for a few uncomfortable moments before speaking. "We'll be with you as soon as possible, but they have a reservation."

He clearly wasn't about to accept that. "First of all, I highly doubt that is possible, since you were clearly surprised to see them a moment ago, and second of all, we have a reservation too, and what's more, it was for ten minutes ago. If you're going to go to the trouble of taking reservations, the least you should do is try to honor them. I demand that we be seated first!"

His tone was so harsh that I had trouble believing it was really happening, though I could understand that most likely at least some of his motivation to act so rudely could be based on the fact that he was probably hungry, not that it was any excuse.

Before Angelica could explode, I said quickly, "Honestly, we don't mind waiting our turn."

Angelica didn't even glance in my direction as I spoke, and I wasn't entirely sure that she'd even heard me. Putting on her sweetest and clearly unfelt smile, she left us for a moment and approached the man in question. As our voluptuous hostess stood over him, I couldn't help but feel a little sorry for him, no matter how rudely he'd just behaved. Angelica could be very sweet, and she usually was, but she couldn't abide rudeness, and the woman had never ignored an instance of it in her life, at least as far as I was aware of. "Sir, this restaurant belongs to me and my daughters, built from humble beginnings to what it is today. When we opened Napoli's, we promised ourselves that our family would always come first, above all else, and these two women are family."

He should have shut up right then and there and cut his losses or even perhaps left to eat somewhere else, but I could tell from the grimly determined set of his jaw that he wasn't going to do either one of those things. "I don't believe that you are related for one second." He looked from me to Grace and then back to Angelica. "They don't look anything like you."

"Michael, it's not important. We can wait until they are ready for us," his dinner date said pleadingly as she tugged at his arm, trying her best to defuse the situation.

"Shut up, Shelly. Simpering doesn't become you. I won't be ignored by some glorified hostess." He then turned back to Angelica and said, "I demand that we be seated immediately."

Angelica shrugged. "My apologies. I'll be glad to take care of you first."

Wow, the smug expression that crossed his face was amazing. He clearly thought he'd won the battle.

I knew he was wrong, but he didn't, at least not yet. Angelica grabbed a pair of menus and instructed them, "If you'll please follow me."

He stood and turned to his date. "Come on. Move it, Shelly. We don't have all evening. I have to get back to the office after we eat, so don't dawdle."

His unfortunate date pursed her lips together and stood, but then, instead of following meekly behind him, she immediately turned to the door to leave.

"Where do you think you're going?" he asked her harshly.

"The second I leave here, I'm going to go kill Helen for setting me up with you in the first place. This is officially the last blind date I'm ever going on in my life. If you're the best that's out there, I'd rather die alone."

"Whatever. It's your loss. You aren't hot enough for me, anyway," Michael said, and then he turned back to Angelica. "Go on. Take me to my table. I don't have much time."

"Follow me, then," Angelica said, and then, almost as an afterthought, she turned to us and added, "You and Grace should wait right here."

"No way is that happening," Grace said with a grin. "We're tagging along with you." It was clear she didn't want to miss the fireworks, and honestly, neither did I.

"As you wish," she said. "Sir? Are you ready?"

"Let's go already," he said in what I'm sure he thought was a commanding and superior tone.

Angelica led him through the dining room straight to the kitchen door, but he clearly didn't realize what was happening, at least not yet, though he clearly did begin to get a little suspicious. "Where are we going?"

"To our special VIP section in back," she said.

"Very good," he answered, still smug about triumphing over Angelica, or so he thought.

As the restaurateur led him through the kitchen door, she called out to her daughters, "Ladies, we have a bad fish among us."

The three lovely DeAngelis daughters present leapt into action as though they had rehearsed their responses a thousand times. Antonia dropped her order pad and picked up a large meat cleaver, Maria snagged a heavy cast iron pan, while Sophia firmed her grip on the ladle in her hands and brandished it as though it were a weapon. It must have been Tianna's day off, or she would have been right there with them.

"What's going on here?" the man demanded, finally realizing that the tables had been turned against him.

"It is important that you listen very carefully and do as you are told," Angelica said to him, the solicitousness gone from her voice. It was clear that she was finished playing around as she threw open the back door that led to the rear of the strip mall where the restaurant was located. "You may leave now."

The man looked outraged. "Let me get this straight. You're throwing me out because I complained about you abusing your tiny little power to bump me from my dinner reservation?"

"If you had taken the time to study the sign posted near the entry, you would have seen that it announces that we reserve the right to serve whomever we choose to serve and refuse service to all others. Now, will you leave quietly, or must I call the police chief, one of my very good customers as well as a very dear friend?"

"You know what? Forget it! I don't want to eat here anymore, anyway," he said. "But I'm not walking out the back door like some kind of vagrant! I'm going out the way I came in."

"Then I wish you luck getting through our little gauntlet," she said, blocking his exit back through the dining room as her daughters closed ranks.

"Through all of us," I said as I picked up a pan of my own. Grace grabbed a two-pronged skewer that looked particularly deadly, and in other circumstances it might have been comical, but things were deadly serious at the moment. I couldn't blame Angelica for her demand. There was no doubt in my mind that if he were allowed to exit through the front, he'd make quite a scene on his way out.

He must have finally realized that it was a lost cause. "Forget it. It's not worth the hassle."

"Good choice," she said, "and for the record, you are not being removed from our restaurant for protesting your waiting time. You are not welcome back here because of the way you treat people. Ever."

"You're banning me?" he asked, clearly outraged by the thought.

"Precisely. You may leave," Angelica said grimly. "Now," she added as she chose a heavy-duty cast iron lid that could inflict some serious damage if needed.

He stalked out without another word, but on his way out, he did manage to slam the back door so hard I thought it might come off the hinges.

Once he was gone, Maria turned to her mother. "What exactly happened out there?"

"He disrespected me and the woman he was with," she replied. "You know how I feel about rudeness."

"That's all we need to know. We had your back, Mom," Sophia said.

"I appreciate that, my dear," Angelica replied gently.

"What were you going to do to him, Sophia, pour some

hot marinara sauce over his head?" Maria asked with a smile. It was clear that all of the DeAngelis women were happy that the tension had been dissipated.

"Hey, I could have done some damage with this. Trust me," Sophia said, waving the ladle around as though it were a fencing sword at first and then converting it into a bludgeon.

Angelica smiled at her youngest daughter and took the ladle from her hands gently. "I'm just happy that it didn't come to that." She turned back to us. "Now, would you two still like that table?" She had noticed our weapons with approval as we put them back where we'd found them.

"If it's all the same to you, I think we'd rather eat back here," I said as I pointed to the table perched in one corner of the kitchen where I'd dined occasionally in the past. As much as I loved the ornately decorated area in front, eating in back actually made me feel as though I was, at least for a moment or two, part of this large, bustling, and very loving family.

"We would love to have you join us," Angelica said, and then she turned to Maria. "Would you mind taking over up front?"

"If I can throw the next rude person out myself, I'd love to," Maria said with a grin. Though she was quite lovely in her own right, her splendor was mere moonlight compared to her mother's sunny beauty.

Angelica said a little ruefully, "I fear I set a bad example for you girls at times."

The restaurant owner was greeted by a sudden flurry of embraces from her beautiful daughters on all sides, and I knew that if any man alive had received such treatment, he would have never been able to get the smile off his face.

"I love you all very much, now get back to work," she said in mock severity.

They instantly broke their grips and did as they had been

instructed. Angelica was a force to be reckoned with, even for those she was closest to.

"Those girls are truly special," she said to us softly, and I noticed a tear tracking down her cheek.

"They love their mother, and with good reason," I replied.

Angelica took a moment to savor the thought, and then she flicked away the last tear. "Now, what should we start with? Ladies, may I choose your menu this evening?"

I knew better than to argue with that suggestion. "Of course," I said as Grace chimed in beside me almost immediately.

"Very well," she said as she rubbed her hands together. "Let me see. I believe we'll start with..." and she was off, planning what was no doubt going to be a feast to remember for Grace and me.

"I couldn't eat another bite at gunpoint," I told Grace as I pushed my plate away. We'd taken a culinary tour of Italy, and I for one was exhausted. For some folks, eating was a competitive sport, and the way Angelica kept adding sample after sample, I wasn't sure the table would stand up under the weight of so much food. It had managed somehow to hold it all though, and Grace and I were both stuffed.

"That was amazing," I told Angelica when she approached offering thirds, "but you've got to stop feeding us. You're killing us with goodness."

"There are worse ways to go, I suppose," Angelica said with a smile, "but the point is well taken. All that's left is that we need to settle up your bill."

"I'm more than happy to pay for this," Grace said. "What do we owe you?"

"A favor," Angelica said as her smile faded away for a moment.

"I can't imagine anything we could do for you that is worthy of the meal we just shared, but we'll do our best. You don't have to bribe us, you know," I said with a grin. "We'll pay for our meal *and* do you the favor. All you have to do is ask. Now, what is it that we can do for you?"

"It's not for me," Angelica answered.

"Is it for one of the girls?" I asked her softly so the daughters couldn't hear us, in case that was what she was getting at.

"No, thank goodness, all of them are fine at the moment, an aligning of the stars that I can hardly believe myself."

"Then what is it?" I asked. Angelica had my curiosity going at full speed, something that admittedly wasn't that hard to trigger. I'd always been an inquisitive child, and it hadn't faded in the years since. If anything, my amateur sleuthing had somehow managed to intensify it to the point where I saw mysteries sometimes where there weren't even any there.

"It's your mayor. I'm worried about him."

"George?" I asked, my smile vanishing as well. "What's going on with him?"

"He was here last night with his lady friend, Cassandra," she explained.

"I don't see that as being a cause for concern," Grace said. "The mayor is allowed to date anyone he pleases, isn't he?"

"Of course he is," Angelica said quickly. "I find him quite handsome myself, and I know under that sometimes gruff exterior beats the heart of a good man."

Was it my imagination, or was Angelica a little sweet on the mayor herself? "You two never thought about dating yourselves, did you?"

Angelica surprised me by turning half a dozen shades of red, something that was rare indeed. "Of course not. Don't be silly."

"Then why the concern?" Grace asked.

"The two of them had quite a row here last night," Angelica said. "I'm not sure what they were fighting about, but it was clear they were both upset by whatever topic they were discussing.

Cassandra stormed out of the restaurant, and George flung four twenties at me as he raced out the door to catch her. It was clearly too much money for their dinner, so I quickly made change and tried to catch up with them in the parking lot before they could leave. I was too late, though. At least to catch Cassandra. Evidently she'd driven them to Union Square, and she left him standing alone in the parking lot with no way to get back to April Springs."

"Wow, that's quite a bit of drama for one night, isn't it?" I asked.

"Things happen in Napoli's sometimes," Angelica said.

"Did you give him a ride home?" Grace asked our hostess with a wicked little grin.

"He had to get back home somehow, didn't he?" she admitted.

"You've got a big heart, Angelica," I said. "Did George happen to talk about what the fight was all about on the drive?"

"He wouldn't say anything specific. I asked him as gently as I could, and all he would say was that some people just couldn't leave well enough alone. I take it she's pushing him hard about something, and she didn't care for his response."

"She wants him to run for governor," Grace said, "and he's clearly not interested in the prospect."

"I didn't realize that. I pushed a little harder, but he wouldn't say a word more about it."

"I believe I have to have myself a little chat with our dear mayor when we get back to town," I said as I glanced at my watch. "Speaking of which, don't forget, I'm supposed to meet Francie Mulligan soon about the giant donut that's being delivered to the shop."

"Pardon me?" Angelica asked. "Why on earth would you have a donut delivered to a donut shop, let alone a giant one?"

"It's for our anniversary celebration," I quickly explained.

"It's a giant fiberglass donut for the shop roof, and Grace has hired Francie to install it for me."

"Fix It Francie has done work for me here," Angelica said with a nod of approval. "You'll speak with George soon, won't you?"

"As soon as humanly possible," I said as I nodded. "That's something I would do anyway after hearing what happened between him and Cassandra. So we still owe you for our meal."

"Nonsense," Angelica said. "Do I charge my own daughters for the food they eat?"

"You made me pay for that cupcake I bought last week," Sophia reminded her. It was no surprise that she'd been listening in to our conversation. After all, the kitchen wasn't that big, and besides, we hadn't made any efforts to keep anything from the girls as they worked.

"That was ridiculous," Angelica told her youngest. "Imagine paying nearly five dollars for one cupcake, no matter how large it might have been. It's unheard of."

"It was awfully tasty though, wasn't it? You really seemed to like the bite you had," Sophia said with a smile.

"Not five dollars' worth," she retorted before turning back to us. "You were saying?"

Grace put a twenty on the table, and Angelica immediately stiffened. "What is that, young lady? Are you trying to insult me?"

"I wouldn't dream of it. That's not for dinner," Grace said in a calm voice.

Angelica looked puzzled by her explanation. "Then what could it possibly be for?"

"Think of it as cupcake money," Grace answered as a grin broke out. "This way you can each get one and enjoy it guilt-free as to what it costs."

Angelica was clearly about to refuse when Sophia walked by and scooped the money up. "Thanks, Grace. We'll do just that."

"We will do no such thing," Angelica answered sternly.

"Let's take a vote," Sophia said as Maria walked in.

"What are we voting on?" she asked us all.

"Grace wants to buy us all cupcakes. All in favor say aye," the youngest daughter said with a smile.

There was a resounding set of yeses given, and Sophia smiled at her mother. "There you go. It's unanimous."

"You didn't ask for nay votes," Angelica reminded her.

"Now why in the world would I want to do that?" the youngest said with a grin.

I could see that Angelica was forming a protest when the frown faded into a smile. "Oh, why not? I know when I'm beaten. Thank you, Grace. It's most generous of you."

"Is that all it takes?" Antonia asked happily. "We need to vote on things more often around here."

"Sorry, but you used your only election this year on cupcakes, of all things."

"If you ask me, it was worth it," Sophia said. "Totally worth it."

CHAPTER 5

"I'M WORRIED ABOUT GEORGE," I told Grace as we headed back to April Springs. We had some time to kill on the drive, and I wasn't about to waste it. "Do you think he's okay?"

"It's been my experience in the past that our mayor can take care of himself," Grace said beside me. I'd felt guilty about not taking my Jeep, since her new supervisor had turned out to be quite a stickler when it came to using her company car for personal business, but she had insisted, so I'd gone along with her chauffeuring me around.

"In most matters, I'd have to agree, but he's fallen harder for Cassandra than any woman he's dated since I've known him. George let her into his heart, and now, when it's starting to go bad, he's feeling the pain."

"You make him sound like some kind of modern sensitive man," Grace said. "Are we talking about the same guy?"

"George Morris might be gruff on the outside, but his heart can still be broken. Don't forget, he almost left town to be with her."

"The key word here is *almost*. I know it's frustrating to see our friend in pain, but what can we do about it? We can't exactly sit Cassandra down and have a conversation with her, can we?" When I didn't answer, Grace added, "Suzanne, you're kidding. Please tell me you're kidding. We're not going to talk to Cassandra, are we?"

"What could it hurt? She needs to know what she's doing to him." I couldn't stand the thought of just standing idly by while someone hurt my friend.

"We need to butt out," Grace said.

"Maybe," I acknowledged. After giving it a few moments of thought, I asked, "What if we happen to casually drop by and have a chat with her? We could at least see what she has to say."

"That sounds an awful lot like meddling to me," Grace replied.

I glanced over at her. "Sorry to bring this up, but since when have *you* been the voice of reason? You're normally the one dragging me into situations like this, not vice versa."

"Maybe I've learned from past experience not to get involved with people's love lives."

"Do you mean like Marybeth?" I asked her, recalling our earlier conversation with the woman at Cheap Cheeps just that afternoon.

"That's different," Grace protested.

"How so?"

"She came to me, remember? Well, maybe I coaxed her a little, but I doubt Cassandra is going to welcome our presence with a smile."

"Then we keep it light and friendly. I wish I had some old donuts to give her."

"That's the key, all right. Ply her with stale cast-offs," Grace said, smiling to show that she was just teasing. It was a point of pride with me not to sell anything over twelve hours old, though I had been known to give away the donuts left over at the end of the day in the spirit of a good cause.

"We could always buy her a pie," I suggested.

"Or a book," Grace chimed in.

"Why would we buy her a book?"

"It makes as much sense as a pie, and besides, we have a bookstore already," Grace said.

"Fair enough, but I heard a rumor that we might be getting our very own pie shop in town soon," I said.

"Really? That's the best news I've had in a while. I love pie!"

"So do I, but Jake has us both beat. If we had the money, I'm pretty sure he'd want to invest in it himself."

Grace patted my arm lightly. "I hate that you're so worried about money."

"I'm not thrilled about it myself, but George's situation takes precedence even over my financial predicament."

Grace turned off the main highway three miles before we hit the April Springs city limits. "So, I'm guessing we're popping in on Cassandra empty-handed."

"You can wait in the car if you'd rather," I said as she pulled up to Cassandra's condo apartment rental, one of several upscale units staggered across the property. They hadn't been there long, and given the entry-point price, I had first wondered if they'd all just sit empty, but sure enough, only one was still for sale or lease in the entire development, and there were signs that more units would be coming soon.

"No, I'm coming with you. I've always said that if they tar and feather you, I want to be just as gooey and fluffy and standing right beside you."

I had to laugh at the image. "I hope it doesn't come to that, but if it does, it's nice to know that I'll have some company."

I took a breath and rang the doorbell. After nearly a full minute, Cassandra came to the door wearing a fluffy bathrobe and a towel on her head wrapping up her lustrous blonde hair. Blast it all, the woman even managed to look elegant and classy stepping out of the shower. Her state of dress, or rather undress, wasn't going to make this conversation any easier. She frowned as she said, "Ladies, I wasn't expecting you."

"We were just coming back from Union Square and we

thought we'd pop in," I said. I kept waiting for her to invite us inside, but no invitation was forthcoming.

"How lovely," Cassandra said, "but as you can see, I'm just getting ready to go out."

I refused to take the hint. "We ate at Napoli's."

Cassandra's expression narrowed a bit. "And you heard about my little disagreement with George. Tell me, are you here to read me the riot act?" She looked equal parts annoyed and amused, which I would have thought previously was impossible. "I assure you that it was nothing."

"You left him standing alone in the parking lot watching you drive away," Grace said. "In my book, that's not nothing." Evidently her policy of staying out of it was officially over.

"George got back just fine on his own, and besides, he needed some time to think."

"About anything in particular?" I asked her.

"I'm not sure what business that is of either of yours," Cassandra said. She was a defense attorney, and from what I'd heard, a really good one, and at that moment I was certain I never wanted to be cross-examined by her.

"George is our friend," I said. "When he's hurt and upset, then so are we."

"What is all the fuss about? I have ambitions for the man. Is that so wrong? He'd make a fine governor, given the proper direction and advice."

"The real question is, does he *want* to be governor?" I asked.

"He doesn't know what he wants. That's why he needs me," Cassandra said with a smug little smile.

"At the moment, it sounds as though he's not too happy with you," Grace said. "What makes you think he's going to sit still and be groomed for a job he doesn't want?"

"He'll do what *I* see fit," she said fiercely, "and what's more, he'll like it."

"I wouldn't be so sure of that," I said. "He's got a mind of his own, and if you don't stop pushing him, you might find yourself on the outside looking in."

"We'll just see about that. Now if you two will excuse me, I don't have time to chat with you about my personal life." Almost as an afterthought, she added, "So lovely of you both to stop by. Next time you might want to call first, though. Good-bye."

With that she closed the door in our faces, leaving us standing on the stoop looking more than a little bit foolish.

"Wow, that's a side of her that I haven't seen before," Grace said as we got back into her company car and headed for town. "She's got a streak of iron and more than a little bit of mean in her, doesn't she?"

"I think it's more like ice," I said. "What does George see in her?"

Grace laughed. "Do you mean besides the fact that she's beautiful, accomplished, successful, and usually pretty charming?"

"Yes, besides all of that," I said, and then I had to laugh. "Grace, am I just being silly?"

"You are not. She's doing her best to manipulate our friend and making him miserable in the process. I wasn't sure that butting in was the right thing to do, but after that conversation, I'm starting to think that maybe George needs us to help extricate him from the situation."

"Only if that's what he wants," I said, reminding her that ultimately it was the mayor's decision.

"Well, he doesn't seem to be too happy with her right now," Grace said.

"The truth is, we've heard a lot of people's opinions today except the one that really matters. Let's go see George."

"What if *he's* the one who Cassandra is meeting?" Grace asked.

"Then it will be the more the merrier, as far as I'm concerned."

"Suzanne, if we both go, George is going to feel as though we are ganging up on him," Grace said a minute later.

"You don't expect *me* not to go, do you?" I asked.

"No. Just the opposite, in fact. You've known him a lot longer than I have, and the two of you have been close for years. As much as I hate to say it, I should probably sit this one out."

I'd been wondering the same thing, but I hadn't wanted to bring it up to Grace. George was going to probably feel attacked as it was. If Grace was with me, there was a pretty good chance that he'd just shut down and refuse to discuss it at all. "As much as it pains me, I agree. Don't worry, though. After we chat, I'll come over and tell you all about it."

She glanced at her watch before she answered. "It's going to have to wait until later. Stephen and I are having a conversation this evening that might take some time."

Grace had been dating our chief of police for some time, but it had been a turbulent relationship at times. Was this nearing the beginning of the end of it? "Just how bad are things between the two of you?"

"I'm not sure. He told me yesterday that we needed to talk, so I suspect that I'm about to be dumped." Grace sounded a bit dead inside when she said it.

I reached over and patted her arm. "I'm so sorry. Is there anything I can do to help?"

"Nothing comes to mind off the top of my head," she said, and then she offered me a sadly sweet smile. "These things happen."

"Far too often, it seems to me," I agreed as we pulled up in front of my cottage, which happened to be less than a hundred yards from her place. As I got out, I said, "Call me when he leaves, no matter how late it might be."

"If I feel like talking," she said as I closed the door. "You understand, don't you?"

"Completely. At least come by the donut shop in the morning. I'll buy you a treat and you can keep me company."

"I might just take you up on that," she said, and then I watched as she drove away, heading back to her big, empty house all alone. It made me grateful yet again that I had Jake, and even though he wasn't there with me physically at the moment, he was in my heart always. I thought about skipping my plans, staying right where I was, changing into my most comfortable pajamas, and watching a movie with my good friends Ben and Jerry, but it took only a moment to realize that George needed me.

Everything else was going to have to wait.

As I drove by the donut shop, I naturally glanced over and saw something I hadn't been expecting, something I'd missed from the passenger side of Grace's luxury automobile. The giant donut had indeed been delivered, and Francie and a man I didn't know were coming down a ladder in front of the shop! The fiberglass donut, in all its glory, was mounted on the roof just above my sign!

I parked the Jeep and hurried toward them.

Before I could say a word, Francie said, "Suzanne, I hope you don't mind, but I decided to take a little initiative and go ahead and put your donut up for you. You didn't show up, and I didn't have your cell phone number."

"I'm sorry. A friend needed me," I said. "I appreciate you doing this without me. How bad was it to get it up there?"

"I'll tell you one thing; that donut was a lot heavier than it looked. I had to call my brother to come help get it up there. Say hello, Frank."

"'Lo," Frank said.

"Nice to meet you," I said as I offered him my hand, which he took for the slightest of seconds. "Thanks so much for your help. Let me pay you for your time, too," I said as I reached for my ever-slimming wallet.

"Nope," he said with a shrug. "We're good."

"Just in case you hadn't noticed, Frank's the real talker in the family," Francie said with a grin. "How does it look?"

"I'm going to have to get a spotlight on it at night," I replied as I took a few steps back and admired it. Grace had been right. It really did add a nice touch to our celebration, and I was even a little sad that I couldn't keep it. What better way to draw folks in than such an obvious advertisement of what I did for a living?

"I can do that for you, too," Francie said.

Remembering the state of my finances, I decided that discretion really might be the better part of valor. "Let me think about it. In the meantime, should I pay you now?" Grace had insisted on covering it, but I was having a hard time letting her pay for the donut rental and its installation, too.

"We're all covered. Grace has already taken care of it," Francie said. "You haven't seen the last of us, though. Frank and I have decided to meet here for breakfast in the morning."

"Then the donuts are on me, above and beyond your fees, and I won't take no for an answer," I said.

Frank grinned broadly. "Cool."

I got back into the Jeep and headed on to George's place as the brother-and-sister team loaded the ladder on the back of Francie's truck. I was happy that I'd found her, but if I had any talents at all, it seemed to be the ability to draw good people to me.

It was better than flying or x-ray vision, at least as far as I was concerned.

"Hey, George. Are you out here waiting for someone?" I'd found my friend sitting out on his front stoop, peering up and down the block, when I'd driven up.

"Cassandra called me. She told me all about your little visit, and she's not very happy about it. Suzanne, I have enough problems with her as it is. I don't need you and Grace hounding her about our relationship, too."

"Do you even have one anymore?" I asked him with a bluntness reserved for my closest friends. "Before you get too upset with us, we weren't just being nosy. Grace and I had dinner at Napoli's this evening."

"And Angelica just had to say something to you," he said with a snort of disgust. "I should have figured that would happen. After all, you two are as thick as thieves."

I sat down on the stoop beside him. "That's because she knows how much I care about you. George, what's really going on? This *all* can't be about you running for governor."

"Cassandra had to have told you that herself, because I'm certainly not spreading the news," George said with a snort. "I told her no, and I meant it. I didn't want to hold public office to begin with, but then you and your mother dragooned me into becoming mayor. I'll admit that I've grown fond of the job, but the idea of me running for statewide office is ridiculous, and I've told her so on numerous occasions. I don't know what she told you, but that wasn't what our fight was about."

That was interesting, since it was the *only* reason Cassandra had given for their tiff. "Then what was it?"

"Have you been following the Harvey Clint Brevard case?" he asked me, his voice suddenly growing leaden.

"He shot two police officers in Manson County," I said. It had been all over the papers, and I knew that his case was coming up for trial soon, but I tended to stay away from bad news in general, and Brevard was all sorts of that as far as I was concerned.

"The dashcam caught the whole thing, but he's still fighting it tooth and nail. Guess who has decided to represent him?"

"Cassandra," I said, not even needing George to confirm it. She'd been a high-profile defense attorney for years, so in a way, it made sense. Still. "And you were a cop long before you ever were the mayor," I said, stating the obvious.

"I can't believe she's doing it. I know that everyone is allowed to get the best defense they can afford, but he's stone broke. She's doing it for free!"

"Well, it's not *entirely* free," I said softly.

"What do you mean?"

Did I really have to say it out loud? "There's going to be a lot more press and publicity about the case than usual, isn't there?"

I expected George to blow up at the suggestion that his girlfriend had taken the case just so she could be in the limelight, but surely that thought had occurred to him before *I'd* brought it up.

His reaction told me that he had indeed considered it. "Of course there is. Cassandra wants to be the bride at every wedding and the corpse at every funeral. She can't stand not being center of attention in April Springs, so she's doing whatever she can to get some of her high profile back." In a voice so soft I could barely hear him, he added, "I wish I'd never asked her to move here."

Wow, that was huge, not only the admission that he'd made a mistake in his love life but that he'd chosen to share it with me. George Morris was not, on the whole, big on opening up his personal life, even to his friends. "What are you going to do?"

"I'm breaking up with her," George said as he slapped his open palms on his thighs. "I'm not about to stay with her, given her decisions of late." He shook his head. "I don't think she's even going to be all that upset. I think she might be seeing someone else on the side, or at the very least thinking about it."

"Oh, George. I'm so sorry." Was that the reason Cassandra had brushed us off? Had she been getting ready for her clandestine tryst? "When are you going to tell her?"

"Soon. Tonight, if possible. After all, there's no point in delaying it. I'd just as soon rip the Band-Aid off and get on with my life."

"If there's anything I can do, you know I will." I had a sudden thought. "Why don't you come by the cottage after you two talk?"

"Don't you have to get up early to make donuts tomorrow morning?" he asked me.

"I do, but since Jake is gone, I can take a nap, so I'll be wide awake when you get there," I said.

"So Jake talked you into letting him take the gig in Virginia," George said.

"You knew about that?" I asked. Why had my husband discussed the job offer with his friend but not with me? I didn't care for that, not one little bit.

"Don't get angry with either one of us. We were eating lunch when he got the call, so naturally we discussed it. He turned it down on the spot, but the guy was pretty insistent. I don't blame him. If I needed someone to watch my back, I can't think of anyone I'd rather have doing it than Jake." The mayor stretched out one knee, and I heard something pop. I hoped that it wasn't from the time he'd been hit with a car by a murderer we'd been trying to nail, but I wasn't about to ask. "I'm a bit surprised that you let him do it. What's going on?"

He'd been so open and honest with me that I couldn't keep

my situation from him. Besides, I knew that George held a great many more secrets in confidence than he would be keeping for me. "The shop's in trouble, and frankly, we need the money."

The mayor took the news in silence, only nodding once upon hearing it. After nearly a full minute, he asked, "Are you going to do something about it?"

"We're having an anniversary party for the donut shop in three days. Hopefully it will remind folks that I'm right here if they get a craving for something sweet."

"Is there anything I can do?" George asked. Even in this troubled time for him, it touched me that he still managed to think of me.

"Do you mean like give a speech or cut a ribbon or something?" I asked him with a grin.

"No, nothing like that," he said with a chuckle. "If I put them to sleep, how are they going to buy your donuts? Anything else I can do, though, I will. All you have to do is ask."

I patted his arm. "Thanks. I appreciate that, but let's get back to you for a second. Will you promise me to come by the cottage after you break up with Cassandra? I mean it, George. If you don't give me your word, I won't leave you alone for one second."

"I promise," he said. "You're probably right. I don't need to be alone. Tell you what. I'll come by, but I'm only going to stay a few minutes. Agreed?"

It wasn't much, but I knew that I was going to have to take it. "Agreed," I said. "Do you want to talk about it in the meantime?"

"No, I believe I'll save our little chat for later," he replied as he stood. I heard a few things creaking again, but I had to wonder if it was more from his age than past injuries he'd suffered. I got up as well, not as quickly as I might have once but still a little easier than he had.

It wasn't much, but at least it was something.

I impulsively kissed his cheek lightly, and when I pulled back, I saw that he was blushing a bit. "Sorry, I couldn't help myself."

"That's me, George Morris, Woman Magnet," the mayor said with a laugh.

As I started to go, I turned back and said, "Remember, I'll be expecting you."

"I won't forget," George said.

I got back in my Jeep and headed to the cottage. I decided that a nap was exactly what I needed, especially if I was going to be alert when George came over later. I put on some soft background music and lay down on the couch, hoping to get a little rest. My mind wasn't cooperating, though. A thousand thoughts kept flooding through my stream of consciousness, from the danger Jake might be in to the dire financial shape of Donut Hearts to George's impending breakup. I grabbed my phone and started to call Jake when I realized that he had enough on his hands at the moment without me adding to his worries. Besides, he'd warned me that he probably wouldn't be able to answer my calls, so I put the phone back on the coffee table and tried to will myself to sleep.

To my amazement, it actually worked.

I woke up abruptly to someone pounding on my front door. Rubbing my eyes with my hands, I glanced at the clock and saw that I'd been asleep for nearly two hours. A groggy feeling washed over me, but the second I opened the door, one look at George's face brought me instantly awake.

"What's wrong, George?"

"It's Cassandra," he said, his face as pale as moonlight.

"She's dead."

CHAPTER 6

"WHAT DO YOU MEAN, SHE'S dead?" I asked him as I shook my head to get rid of the cobwebs still there. "What happened?"

"Come with me and I'll show you," George said, pulling at my arm.

"Where are we going?"

"To Donut Hearts," he replied as he started off toward the nearby park on foot.

"George, why are we going there?"

"I was supposed to meet Cassandra out in front of your shop twenty minutes ago," he said, his breathing ragged as he pushed ahead.

"And did you?" I asked, wondering where this was leading.

"I showed up, and when I did, that's where I found her," George answered, his voice coming out loudly due to the stress he was clearly under at the moment.

"Did you at least call Stephen Grant before you came and got me?" I asked. "The police chief needs to know what's going on."

"I wanted to show her to you first," he said as we neared the shop.

"I don't care what you think, I'm calling him," I said as I took out my cell phone.

George grabbed my arm in a strong grip that actually hurt. "Don't do that, Suzanne."

"Let go of me, George! That hurts!" I said a more shrilly than I probably should have.

He must have realized how strong his grip on me was, because he let go immediately. In a softer voice, he pointed to something large on the ground, barely in the shadows of the streetlight down the road.

It was the giant fiberglass donut that had so recently been poised on my roof.

Somehow it had fallen from its high perch, which was bad enough, but the damage to the rental was the least of our problems.

Cassandra Lane was lying underneath it, pinned facedown on the sidewalk by the giant decorative donut.

Taking in the scene, I wasn't sure that I'd ever be able to eat one again.

As I knelt down to search for a pulse, George said, "Don't bother. I already checked for it. She's dead."

He was right about that. I couldn't find one, but that didn't necessarily mean that a faint one wasn't present, something that we civilians might not have been able to determine.

I stood and pulled my phone out, stepping away and glaring at the mayor as I did so. "I'm calling Stephen, and don't try to stop me."

George shook his head, and then he slumped down, nearly falling onto the nearby chair where some folks liked to eat their donuts out in the sunshine. "I won't fight you anymore," he said weakly.

Thank goodness the chief picked up on the third ring. His tone of voice surprised me, though. "If you're looking for Grace, I left her place an hour ago."

I had forgotten they were going to have a talk this evening. Too much else had been going on.

"Actually, I need to speak with you. You need to get over here to the donut shop right away. There's been an accident." At least I *thought* it was an accident. After all, what were the odds that someone would plan to murder Cassandra Lane by pushing a fiberglass donut off my roof and killing her?

"Did someone get hit by a car?" he asked. I could hear him grabbing his keys, so I had a hunch that he was either at home or at the station. Either way, he was mere minutes away.

"Cassandra Lane was crushed by a giant donut," I said. It had even sounded insane as I'd said it, but it was the truth, and there was no other way to put it as far as I was concerned.

"Suzanne, that's not even a little bit funny."

"It wasn't meant to be," I explained in a harsh voice. "A giant donut I had mounted on the roof this evening broke free and landed on Cassandra. George is here with me, and we couldn't find a pulse, but that doesn't necessarily mean that she doesn't have one."

"Boy, I hope you paid up your insurance. I'll be right there. Don't worry about calling for an ambulance. I'll take care of that myself."

"Thanks, Chief."

"I'm on my way," he said, and then he cut the connection.

I moved near George and took the seat beside him. "He's coming right now."

The mayor, my friend, had his head in his hands. He barely looked up as I told him the news. "Good. That's fine. Suzanne, I can't believe this happened."

"I can't, either," I said. "Are you going to be okay?"

"Spare me the sympathy. We both know that I was breaking up with her," George said. "I'm just glad she wasn't murdered."

"What makes you say something like that?" I asked him, even though I'd thought the same thing myself when I'd first seen her body pinned under the fiberglass.

"I'm truly sorry that she's dead, but it could have been bad for me. We haven't exactly been getting along lately."

"Still, you've been close for a long time, and I'm sorry that it happened."

"So am I," he said as the chief's cruiser came roaring up. He slammed it into a spot in front of my shop and got out on the fly. When my stepfather had been the police chief, he'd never run anywhere. It was nice having a younger chief, at least when it came to being fit. I hadn't given Phillip a lot of credit when he'd been running things, but it turned out that he had been better at his job than I'd ever thought at the time. Hindsight truly is twenty-twenty in some cases.

Chief Grant ignored us and headed straight for the body.

"You won't find a pulse," George told him. "We both already tried."

The chief ignored us and continued to search for some faint flicker of life.

Ten seconds later, the ambulance came. I found myself hoping that they'd be able to do anything but cart off the dead body, but I strongly doubted it. There was a phone call I had to make, but I really didn't want to do it. I knew that I needed to reach out and tell Francie what had happened before she heard about it from someone else. She was going to feel horrible about this, and I had to wonder if she might have been criminally negligent when she and her brother had installed the donut. After all, it couldn't have just fallen on its own.

At least I didn't think so. I just couldn't bring myself to make the call.

The EMTs arrived and quickly confirmed our opinions.

Cassandra Lane was, now and forever, beyond anyone else's help.

It surprised me a little when I realized that the arriving backup police officers were treating it like a crime scene, taking photos and video before they moved the donut off of Cassandra's body. The chief had asked George and me to stay, which we did, although we'd moved to a bench in the park just across the street. There would be time for our stories later. Right now, everything was being documented.

Finally, the chief nodded to two of his men, who gently lifted the donut off of Cassandra's lifeless body. For a woman with so much life in her, so much personality, she looked tiny in death, fragile, which, in the end, I realized we all were. I knew that death was a part of life, but I hated the thought of someone's time on earth cut short so abruptly and unexpectedly. They got more footage after the body was taken away, and finally, one of the maintenance men for the town showed up with a ladder on the back of his truck.

"What's going on, Chief?" I asked from where we sat.

"I'm going up on the roof," he said.

"In the dark? What do you expect to see up there?"

He held up a large flashlight that was standard police issue. "I won't be long."

"Can we go back to my cottage now?" I asked. "You can just as easily speak with us there." George was edging into shock, and I wanted to get him away from the donut shop.

"Just give me a few more minutes," Chief Grant said as he instructed the worker to place the ladder against the front of the building.

As the chief climbed up and then stepped off the ladder and onto the roof, I saw a familiar truck approach. It was Francie! I had planned on telling her what had happened, but I hadn't been ready to make that troubling call just yet, and now it was out of my hands.

"What happened, Suzanne?" she asked as she got out and approached us, taking in the scene. "Why did you take the donut off the roof? If you didn't like where I placed it, you could have called me and I would have done it for you. There was no reason to get the police involved, for goodness sake." She sounded hurt, almost accusing me of doing it without her.

I was about to tell her as gently as I could what had happened when George blurted out, "Your donut rolled off of the roof and killed my girlfriend."

"Excuse me?" Francie asked, clearly confused by what the mayor had just told her.

"I said that it fell off the roof and crushed her," George said woodenly. The mayor really was in shock.

"That's impossible," Francie protested, staring at the donut as though it had suddenly come to life and had committed homicide.

"You didn't see her body pinned under it," George said. "She didn't have a chance."

Francie turned to look at me, tears rolling down her cheeks. "Suzanne? Is that really true?"

"I'm afraid so," I said. "Cassandra is dead."

Francie stumbled for a moment, and if I hadn't jumped up and grabbed her, she would have collapsed on the spot. "I don't understand. That thing should have stayed up there in a hurricane. I would have bet anything that the roof would have flown off before the donut could come down."

"You can't blame yourself. Accidents happen," I said.

"Not to me they don't," she answered as the chief came hurrying down the ladder.

"What did you find up there?" I asked him, but he ignored me as he ran around the other side of my shop. "Rick. Darby. Follow me."

Two of his subordinates did as they were told, but I noticed that Darby looked as though he was going to throw up, as he had arrived on the scene just a minute before. I could understand that reaction from a civilian, but he had surely been around death before. And yet he could barely pull his gaze away from where Cassandra's dead body had recently been. Still and all, he responded to his boss's orders and followed him.

The three of them were back within a minute.

"Are you going to tell us what's going on?" I asked him as I got in the police chief's face.

"Someone tampered with those wires," he reported. "They were cut clean through, and there's a ladder in the weeds behind your shop. I suspect someone deliberately tampered with that donut, and when Cassandra got into the right position, they snipped the last wire and pushed."

Francie seemed to melt a little. "My knots were good, then?"

"They're perfectly intact," the chief said.

Francie's brother pulled up and joined us. "What's going on here?"

After the handywoman brought him up to date, he put an arm around his sister. "Let's get you out of here." It was the most I'd ever heard him speak before. "Can she go, Sheriff?"

"It's Chief, as a matter of fact," he corrected him, but then Stephen nodded. "You are both free to leave." He sounded a bit officious as he said it, and he must have realized it, because he quickly added, "Ma'am, none of this was your fault."

She seemed comforted by his words, and as Frank led her away, he said, "Don't worry, little sister. We'll come back and get your truck later."

"I can drive myself," Francie insisted, pulling against his gentle grip.

"Sure you can. Just indulge me this one time though, okay?"

At last, she seemed grateful to have him there. "Thanks, bro."

"You're welcome," he replied as he squeezed her shoulder. It made me wish I hadn't been an only child. Then again, I'd had friends who had hated their siblings growing up and still didn't speak to them in adulthood. I supposed that it was a mixed bag, and like anything else, it depended on the people involved. Still, I had Grace, and she was as close to a sister as I ever needed.

"What about us?" I asked the chief. "Do you need us at this very second?" I didn't want George at the scene of Cassandra's murder any more than Frank had wanted his sister there.

"I'm afraid I need to speak with you both before you go anywhere," the chief said. "Tell me everything, and start from the beginning."

"Suzanne wasn't a part of this," George said. "I dragged her into it."

Chief Grant looked surprised by the information, perhaps remembering the times in the past that I'd been a part of other homicides in our fine little town. "Is that true?"

"George came and got me at the cottage," I said. "When we got here, I saw Cassandra's body and I called you. End of story."

The chief looked at his boss askance. "You didn't call me first, Mayor?"

George looked embarrassed as he admitted, "I panicked. I was supposed to meet Cassandra here, but when I got to Donut Hearts, she was already dead."

"And despite the fact that you were a trained police officer for many years, you neglected to report a dead body and decided instead to leave a potential crime scene and ask a civilian to join you here before notifying the authorities."

"You don't have to be so hard on him," I chided the chief.

Before he could answer, George did it for him. "Suzanne, he's right. If I were investigating this, I'd be suspicious of me too, and I *know* that I didn't do it."

It was clear the chief hadn't appreciated me jumping to George's defense. "Perhaps we'd both be more comfortable talking about this in my office, Mr. Mayor."

"You shouldn't go anywhere without an attorney," I warned George.

"Who would I call, Suzanne? My lawyer was just murdered, remember?" He looked as though he wanted to die himself, and I was genuinely worried about my friend. "Let's go, Chief."

"Will I be able to open my donut shop tomorrow?" I asked him. I might not get much more sleep, but at least I'd taken a nap.

"I don't see why not," he said. "I'm kind of surprised you'd want to, though."

"Believe me, I'm not happy about it, but I can't afford to lose a single day of sales if it can be at all helped," I admitted.

"You should be fine. If we need anything up on the roof after you open, we'll put our ladders in back, so it shouldn't disturb your customers. There should be room enough to let people in the front, but there's going to be crime scene tape pretty close to it. I'm sorry, but there's nothing I can do about that. We have to follow strict procedures now that we know this is a homicide."

"I understand. If it keeps folks away, there's nothing I can do about it, but I at least have to try."

"Okay. I'll see you later, then." After giving instructions to a few of his officers, the chief turned to George and asked, "Are you ready to come along with me?"

"I've got nowhere else to go," he said in a defeated voice that nearly broke my heart.

As they got into the squad car, I was at least thankful that the chief allowed George to ride up front with him instead of in the back like some kind of criminal.

Unfortunately, when I got to Grace's house, her car was gone. Just to be sure, I rang the doorbell, but there was no answer. I had to wonder if she'd taken off because of the talk she and Stephen had shared or if it was somehow work related. Things happened with her sometimes that way. She'd be sailing along smoothly, managing the cosmetics reps under her and generally being left alone by her supervisor, but every now and then she would have to drop everything and take off at a moment's notice, especially when her boss was replaced, which happened more often than I ever would have imagined. The cosmetics business must have been a great deal more cutthroat than my line of work.

I fought a yawn as I walked the rest of the way back to my cottage. I hated that George was with the police chief, but there was nothing I could do about it, at least not at the moment. I glanced at my phone to check the time since I'd left my watch at home, and I saw that I'd have to be at work in less than three hours. I wasn't about to throw that time away. If I could sleep for at least half that time until I was due to get up for the day, I'd count it as a win.

I didn't even think about calling Jake, as much as I would have loved to hear the sound of his voice.

There was just too much I didn't want to get into.

I was glad that I had set my alarm. Otherwise I would have slept right through it and April Springs would have been donutless, since I was working a few more days alone. It wasn't for any fiscal reason this time, though; Sharon and Emma were taking a little trip together, and what was more, they'd convinced Emma's dad, Ray, to go with them. It was probably going to be the last vacation that Ray Blake, the owner of the newspaper, ever took. I couldn't imagine how he'd react when he got back to town and found out that Cassandra Lane had been killed by a giant donut, of all things. If he'd been home and working, the banner headline would surely have filled the entire front page.

When I got to work, I saw that the chief had been correct in his assessment. There was indeed crime scene tape all around my front door, but it didn't block me or my customers from going inside Donut Hearts. There was even some of the bright-yellow tape draped on the roof, though who would try to go up there was beyond me. Then again, knowing how nosy some of my fellow townsfolk could be, it was probably a good idea to mark it as off limits at that.

I flipped on a few lights as I walked in, switched on the fryer to allow it to warm up, and then hit the coffee urn's power switch. It was a routine I could do practically in my sleep, and as groggy as I was at the moment, it was a good thing.

As I started working on my master cake donut recipe— one that I would divide later and blend into several distinct flavors—I pondered what I knew about Cassandra Lane and, more importantly, who might want to kill her. She had an aggressive personality, there was no doubt about that, and not everyone had found her nearly as charming as George had initially. I knew for a fact that there were some folks in town who might have been tempted to drop a giant donut on her head. One example was Marybeth's reaction the day before at Cheap Cheep's. She'd clearly had problems with the woman on a personal level, and besides George, I was certain that with a little digging, I'd be able to find others Cassandra had managed to infuriate. Then there was her professional life. While death by donut might seem a little strange, the killer had been crafty using what was at hand. Cassandra had made her living and her reputation defending people accused of some pretty heinous crimes, and by the law of averages, at least some of them had probably been guilty. The ones who'd gone to jail despite her best efforts might have come back for a taste of revenge on their attorney, while I could see victims of the killers she'd gotten off might want to exercise a little justice of their own.

I was glad I lived in the world of donuts. Practically nobody ever wanted to kill me because I was featuring apple-stuffed donuts or because I was out of lemon-filled ones.

I finished the master batter and divided it up into smaller portions as I tried to decide what special treat I might offer today. There was a host of regular cake donuts I made nearly all of the time, but every now and then I liked to shake things up. I decided to make an orange marmalade donut with extra orange flavoring as today's treat. Why not? At this point, I really had nothing to lose, and I happened to have a mostly full jar of marmalade in the fridge that I'd just brought from home. Jake had thought it was too sweet to eat, but I thought it would be perfect as a donut additive.

Once the cake donuts were fried and iced, I mixed my yeast dough and took my break as it went through its first rest. I wasn't really sure that I wanted to take my break outside, given what had happened so recently and so tragically out there, but I couldn't let it keep me locked inside.

Those breaks were the moments I missed Emma most when she wasn't working alongside me, not the extra time it took me to wash the pots, pans, utensils, and other things I dirtied. Our conversations sitting outside in front of Donut Hearts, no matter what the weather or time of year, were treasured little memories for me, a part of what made my shop feel so special.

I'd expected to be alone, but that wasn't how it turned out. To my surprise, someone was outside waiting for me.

I nearly screamed when I saw a movement in the shadows out of the corner of one eye and began to regret locking the door to the shop behind me when I'd come out.

CHAPTER 7

"**G**EORGE, WHAT ARE YOU DOING here? Have you even been to bed yet?" I asked the mayor as he stepped forward into the light coming from inside the donut shop. I didn't have much turned on inside, but in the darkness of the night, it still provided plenty of illumination outside.

"I just had to come back here where it happened," George said as he kept staring at the spot where Cassandra had died. The body was gone, as well as the donut. The police had confiscated it, along with the severed wires that had once held it in place. I wasn't sure what Grace was going to tell the rental company, but I knew that she'd handle it with her usual aplomb.

"Are you okay?"

After a momentary pause, he said, "I still can't believe she's dead."

"I'm sure. You've got to be in shock. It's just sinking in, isn't it? Why don't you come inside and have some coffee. I made some cake donuts too, and they are ready to eat, still piping hot."

"Thanks anyway, but I can't bring myself to eat anything," he said.

That was not healthy for him. I took the mayor's arm and lightly guided him toward the front door. "Come in with me and keep me company. I don't really want to be alone, either." I figured if I put it that way, he'd be much more likely to do it.

"I guess I could come in for a minute," he said reluctantly.

"Great," I replied, adding a little more enthusiasm than I normally would. He took a seat at the counter, and I poured us each a cup of coffee. "What kind of donut would you like?"

"Do you have any old-fashioned ones?" he asked.

"You know it. It's one of my best sellers. I'll be right back." As I headed for the kitchen door, I turned back and grinned at him. "Don't you go anywhere now, you hear?"

"No, ma'am. I won't."

I believed him, but I also knew that he was a flight risk at the moment, so I didn't dawdle as I collected two donuts from a tray, one for George and one for me. I couldn't exactly make him eat alone, not that I needed an excuse to eat one of my own treats. I had the curvy figure to prove that had never been an issue for me.

Thankfully, George was still sitting there when I got back forty-five seconds later. I slid one plate in front of him and put another just beside him. Grabbing my cup of coffee, I walked around and joined him as though we were just a pair of customers enjoying a donut together instead of what was really happening. I took a bite of the warm donut, the icing still a bit tacky to the touch, and savored the taste explosion. How could something so simple and inexpensive made with relatively common ingredients manage to taste so good? I was glad it did. It was my business model after all, but sometimes I liked to remember just why I made donuts for a living.

George nibbled on his donut and then took a shallow sip of coffee.

When he didn't make another move to get a second bite, I asked, "Is the donut okay?"

"What? Oh, it's perfect." He sounded as distracted as I'd ever heard him before in my life.

"George, how did it go with Chief Grant?"

For a dozen heartbeats I didn't think the mayor was going to answer, but I was going to give him every second that he needed. After all, this was a difficult subject we were dancing around, so if he needed to sort out his thoughts a bit, I had time. Well, at least nine minutes, since that was all that was left on my timer until it was time to start back on the yeast donuts I needed to make and have ready to sell by the time I opened for business.

I was about to prod him gently when he said, "Suzanne, I'm in some serious trouble here."

"George, I know you didn't do it," I said as reassuringly as I could.

"You're not the one I'm worried about. The chief is pretty suspicious of me, to say the least, and the truth is, if I had been working the case back when I was a cop, I'd think it was a slam dunk. I had plenty of motive, since lots of folks in town have heard Cassandra and me fighting. She wasn't exactly shy about showing her feelings, you know. As to means, I'm not too old to climb a ladder and cut a few wires, and to make matters worse, I knew she was going to be here, since I was the one she was supposed to be meeting. As to opportunity, after you left my place, I drove out to the lake to my house out there and tried to clear my thoughts. Nobody saw me there, and I didn't see a soul, either. The first person I spoke with after you came to my place was you again when I rang your doorbell after I found Cassandra's body."

"All of that is just circumstantial, though," I said, trying to ease his mind a little, though I doubt it had much impact on his mood at the moment.

"There's something else you don't know about," he added, his voice ragged from the strain.

"There's *more?*" I asked him, having a hard time keeping the incredulity out of my voice. What else could there possibly be?

"The chief told me that if I tried to investigate Cassandra's murder, he was going to lock me up, and he meant it. Here I am, looking guilty as original sin, and I can't even do anything to clear my own name." He paused a beat, and then he added, "If Jake were here, I'd ask for his help, but since he's not, I need you, Suzanne. Can you dig into this for me?"

I wasn't insulted that I wasn't his first choice. He would have been insane to come to me before asking Jake for help if my husband had been in town. As a matter of fact, I was honored that I'd come in second. "Of course I'll help you. When have I ever turned my back on a friend?"

"Not as long as I've known you," George said. Was it my imagination, or did his shoulders pick up a little as he said it? "Thanks, Suzanne." Almost as an afterthought, he added, "You're not doing this alone, are you?"

"No, I'm going to see if Grace is free. We're a good team, and we've had a lot of luck in the past." That was certainly true enough. Grace and I had often worked cases together, and it was nice that my best friend also happened to be one of my favorite amateur sleuthing buddies.

"And if she's not available?" George pushed.

"I could always ask Momma or Phillip," I said. I'd worked with my mother and my stepfather on a few occasions, and they each brought their own unique take on our investigations.

"Okay, then," George said. "I won't worry about you, as long as you don't do this alone." With that, the mayor took another and much more substantial bite of his donut and washed it down with a healthy slug of coffee. "You want to know something? I feel better already." He yawned once, fought it, and then yawned again. "Now if you'll excuse me, I need to get to bed. I don't know how you do it each and every night," he said as he stood and automatically reached for his wallet.

"Put that away," I said. "It's not that bad. You get used to it after a while."

"Is that really true?" George asked me.

"No, not really," I replied, adding a laugh and a smile at the end. "I love it, anyway."

"You must," George said. "Thanks for the donut, the coffee, and most of all for stepping up to help me. I can't tell you how much I appreciate it, Suzanne."

"What are friends for?" I asked him as I walked him to the door. "Now go get some sleep and try not to worry so much."

"If only I could," he said with the hint of a wry smile.

After the mayor was gone, I started working the raised dough. First I needed to prep it to be rolled out, then to cut it with my old-fashioned rolling donut cutter, let it spend a little more time rising, and then finally go into the fryer before I iced the results. The process gave me a chance to ponder, to contemplate, and to think about the best way to attack the problem. My movements were all from muscle memory as I did my best to come up with a plan to figure out who had murdered the local attorney.

Unfortunately, I was nowhere closer when it was time to open the shop a few hours later, but at least I had two types of fresh donuts, cake and raised, for sale.

My customers would be happy with fresh treats to tackle a brand-new day.

I only hoped that Grace was free to help me and that we'd be able to come up with some plan to clear George's good name, but the only way we were going to do that was to hunt down and expose Cassandra Lane's killer.

"Are you open for business, Suzanne?" Gabby Williams asked as she walked into Donut Hearts a little after eight that morning. Unfortunately, it was a fair question. Evidently the murder had put an even bigger damper on my already dismal sales, and I'd had just a few customers in the shop since I'd thrown the front door open. If I didn't find the killer and manage to generate a little more foot traffic in my store, I was going to be in dire trouble.

"Yes, of course I'm open. Things are just a little slow at the moment. How's your business doing these days?" Gabby owned ReNEWed, a gently used upscale clothing shop next door to me.

"The truth of the matter is that I'm thinking about cutting my hours back," she said.

"Is business really that bad?" I asked, getting ready to commiserate with her over our mutual financial slumps.

"Quite the contrary. I'm in very real danger of running out of goods to sell I've been so busy lately. It's a real dilemma."

"I just bet it is," I said, trying to keep the envy out of my voice.

"Suzanne, you need to take some proactive measures to keep your business afloat," she answered in that scolding voice of hers.

"I'm trying, but I can't *make* people want my donuts," I said. "Having Cassandra Lane murdered at my front door hasn't helped matters, either."

"I thought when calamity came to your shop, the ghouls came out in force to see the sight for themselves. Don't tell me they've deserted you as well."

"What can I say? Things are slow. I was going to throw an anniversary party for the donut shop in a few days, but I'm not sure I should even go forward with it now."

"Nonsense. That's *exactly* what you must do. Let them all see that you won't be cowed by something like murder."

"That might be easier said than done at the moment," I admitted.

Gabby took a moment before she spoke again, and when she did, the hard edge was gone from her voice, replaced by a more sympathetic tone I didn't experience that much from her. "Suzanne, is there anything I can do to help?"

"Unless you're in the mood for eleven dozen donuts, I'm not sure there is anything anyone can do," I said, glancing back at my display case. If this kept up, I'd wildly overestimated the number of treats I was going to be able to sell that day, and it wasn't like they were widgets, able to last more than a scant few hours. At the end of every business day, I either donated, or worse yet threw out, my leftover inventory. There may have been donut shops in the world that sold day-old donuts, but mine wasn't one of them. I'd rather go broke and out of business before I tried to peddle less-than-perfect treats to the world at large.

"Sorry," she said. "I could take a dozen, though. My customers might appreciate a treat."

"I don't want to guilt you into doing something you wouldn't ordinarily do," I answered.

"As if you could ever do anything like that, dear girl," she said. "Give me your worst-selling donuts and I'll be on my way."

"Of course," I said as I folded a box to prepare her order. It took a second for what she'd said to sink in. "Hang on. Did you just say my worst ones?"

"I did. Why should you waste your bestsellers on me? I'll take the dogs you always have trouble selling. After all, I'm doing my best to give you every chance of a boost."

"I appreciate that," I said, trying to keep my voice calm. After all, she *was* trying to do me a favor, even if she had couched it in terms that I might not be in the mood to accept graciously. "I'll give you choices I'm stocked up in so no one will miss their favorites. After all, I don't sell *any* donuts that aren't delicious."

"Of course you don't," she said as she handed me the money. "Keep the change."

I was willing to sell donuts that might not be as desirable as some, but I wasn't about to accept charity. "Thanks, but I don't think so."

Gabby took the change from me and frowned. "Young lady, you are growing more and more like your mother every day."

"You realize of course that you've just given me the greatest compliment you could ever pay me," I said.

Gabby just shrugged it off. I knew she was a big fan of my mother's as well, but I also realized that it would have pained her to admit it aloud.

Ten minutes after she was gone, I started getting a stream of several other small-business owners in April Springs, each buying a dozen or even two of my donuts. Paige Hill came in, so I finally got the nerve to ask her to confirm my suspicions. "Did Gabby Williams put you up to this?"

"What's that?" Paige asked, trying and failing to look innocent.

"Buying donuts," I said, not giving her a break.

"She might have mentioned that you could use a little help today," Paige admitted, "but I really did need donuts. I've got a new book club meeting at the shop. You should join. It's called Mysteries and Old Maids."

"If you aren't playing the children's game, that might be a bit offensive to some of your members," I said as I put together the requested donuts. My book club had disbanded after an untimely murder, and I wasn't sure it would ever meet again. I had given the donut ordering some consideration since I'd first noticed the pattern of buyers. It wasn't charity, after all, more like a thoughtful gesture by my friends. I knew it was a temporary measure, but at least it would get me through the day, and for that, I was grateful.

"Don't blame me for that name," Paige said, laughing. "The

group insisted upon it. I wanted to call it something else, but the ladies overruled me. There are nine widowed or unmarried women in the group, but the only requirements are that you have to be female, a mystery lover, single, and over the age of seventy. They're even having T-shirts made up."

"That I've got to see," I said as I handed her change to her along with the donuts. "Thanks for doing this."

"Suzanne, you've extended your friendship to me since I opened the shop," Paige said. "This is the least I can do. Oh, and if you need help with your anniversary party, just let me know."

"How did you know about that?" I asked her and then realized I knew the answer already. "Gabby told you."

"Yes, and I think it's an excellent idea. When is it?"

"Day after tomorrow," I answered. I'd decided that Gabby was right. I owed it to Donut Hearts to continue to move forward with my party plans, despite the homicide. After all, I was trying to save my business from the brink of destruction, so I had to force myself to be a little callous about Cassandra's murder. If I could solve it before the party, so much the better, but the celebration had to go on, no matter what my personal feelings about its appropriateness might be.

"Call me if you need me," Paige said on her way out the door.

"You bet," I said as I turned to put the money in the register.

As my back was turned, someone else managed to sneak into the shop. Maybe things were picking up after all.

When I turned back to see who was paying me a visit, I saw that it was Marybeth Jenkins standing there and looking obviously shaken by something.

"What's wrong, Marybeth?" I asked her as I stepped around the counter.

"I keep waiting for the police to show up at my door," she

said, her voice a jangle of nerves. "We're in the same building, for goodness sakes, so why haven't they questioned me about Cassandra's death?"

"If you want to speak with them, maybe you should volunteer and not wait for them to come to you," I suggested.

"I'm assuming that you told them about our conversation at Cheap Cheep, didn't you?" Marybeth asked.

The truth was that I'd considered sharing it with Chief Grant, but he didn't appear to be in a very receptive mood toward my ideas at the moment. "I haven't said anything yet," I said.

"Which means that you're going to," she said, her shoulders slumping visibly. "Suzanne, you know me. I didn't kill her."

"Marybeth, I *do* know you, but that doesn't necessarily mean that you *didn't* do it." I could see her tense up, so before she could blow up at me, I quickly continued, "I'm not accusing you of anything, but in your own words, you said that you wanted what Cassandra had, which was the mayor's heart."

"So, Grace told you all of it, did she? Why am I not surprised? Suzanne, I told her that in confidence."

"Come on, it wasn't a real shock to hear that you've had a crush on the mayor since he first got elected. What I don't understand is why you didn't do anything about it before Cassandra came along. George has dated a few women since he was elected. Didn't you ever think to tell him your true feelings, Marybeth?"

She looked again as though she was about to cry. "It's easy for you, Suzanne. You're pretty and smart and brash. I've got brains, but not the rest of it. I couldn't stand the thought of the mayor rejecting me." It was a sobering commentary not on George Morris but on our clerk of court.

"First of all," I said as gently as I could manage, "it's *never* been easy for me. Second, you are every bit as pretty as I am, and third, I suspect you're smarter than I could ever hope to be.

The brashness just comes from being brave. You know the best definition of bravery I've ever heard? It defines it as courage in the face of fear. It's *okay* to be afraid. You just can't let it run your life." Ordinarily I would never dream of lecturing someone, but Marybeth needed it, at least in my opinion.

"I was braver than you know," Marybeth said, her voice nearly a whisper.

"Did you finally talk to George about your feelings?" I asked her.

"In hindsight, that's probably what I should have done, but instead, I saw Cassandra standing in front of your shop on my way to ReNEWed, so I stopped the car, got out, and I told her that she wasn't good enough for the mayor and that if she didn't step aside, I was going to make sure they were history."

"Oh, no," I said, suddenly fearful that Marybeth might have actually done something to the attorney. "How did she react to what you said?"

"She laughed in my face!" Marybeth said. "Cassandra had the nerve to shoo me away as though I was some kind of pesky insect bothering her. She said that she was there to meet someone important, someone who actually counted!"

"That must have made you furious," I said, realizing that I might be about to hear the confession of a killer without even provoking the admission.

"It made me ashamed," Marybeth said, the tears coming on in full force. "I ran to my car, got in, and drove away as fast as I could. I was so out of it that I nearly ran some poor woman down in the road who was out jogging! Suzanne, Cassandra saw that I wasn't a threat, and it killed my soul to be so exposed like that. I must have driven around half the night trying to compose myself. When I got back into town, I heard that she was dead, killed right out there," she said as she gestured to my storefront. "Exactly where we had our fight."

"Do you know *how* she was murdered, Marybeth?" I asked her, curious as to how much of the real story she had gotten.

"I just assumed that somebody shot her or maybe stabbed her with a knife," she said.

"I'm afraid that it was nothing as ordinary as all that. Someone cut the wires of the display donut on the roof of the shop, and then they pushed it over on top of her."

It took a few moments for that to sink in. "Well, it wasn't me. I'm afraid of heights! You can ask anybody."

"I'm sure the police will make a full inquiry once you speak with them," I said. "But I meant what I said earlier. It will go a great deal easier on you if you approach the police chief and tell him everything that happened yesterday evening. Can you do that?" I looked around the shop, and without any real surprise, I saw that it was completely deserted. "I can shut Donut Hearts and go with you if you think that would help."

"No, I appreciate the offer, but I need to do this myself. Thank you, Suzanne."

"You're very welcome," I said, and then I reached out and squeezed her hand. "You're braver than you realize."

"I only wish that were true," she said. I watched as she got into her car and started for city hall, but instead of pulling into the parking lot, to my surprise, she accelerated and drove past at a furious pace.

Was she actually trying to run away?

There was only one thing I could do, as much as I hated to do it.

I grabbed my cell phone and called Chief Grant. After all, he deserved to know what was going on, and if Marybeth wasn't going to tell him, then I was going to have to do it for her.

"Chief, do you have a second?" I asked when I called him. It helped having his direct line and not having to go through the switchboard, but then again, Stephen Grant and I had been friends since he'd first joined the force.

"Just that, and not much more," he said. "What's up?"

"You need to find Marybeth Jenkins," I told him.

"I didn't realize she was even lost," he said with a hint of humor in his voice. It was frankly nice to hear. Since Stephen had become our chief of police, his playful side had diminished quite a bit. I understood that the weight and responsibility of his job could take a toll on him, but the man seemed to rarely smile anymore, let alone laugh. I had a hunch that was one of the problems Grace was having with him, and I had to wonder yet again how their conversation had gone the night before. I wasn't about to ask the chief, though. If Grace wanted me to know, she would tell me. Otherwise, I was going to do my best to butt out of their relationship, as hard as that was going to be for me.

I hated to break his light mood, but there was nothing I could do about it. "She and Cassandra had a fight yesterday in front of the donut shop not long before Cassandra was murdered."

"Talk to me," Chief Grant said tersely, the former joy gone from his voice in an instant. Once I brought him up to speed, he asked me, "And you don't have any idea where she was headed?"

"I honestly thought she was coming to see you. If I had to guess, I'd say she was on her way to Union Square and points beyond if you don't manage to stop her."

"I'm on it," he said, and without another word, he hung up on me.

So much for exchanging pleasantries. A part of me had hated ratting Marybeth out to the police, but she'd promised to speak with the chief and then she'd clearly changed her mind at the last second. My threat to call the police hadn't been a bluff, so she'd honestly given me no choice.

Even though all of that was true, why did I still feel so badly about it?

CHAPTER 8

"WOW, YOU'VE HAD MORE THAN your share of bad luck lately, haven't you? I can't believe that lawyer was murdered just outside your shop last night," Annabeth Kline said after walking into Donut Hearts twenty minutes before I was due to close. I wasn't even sure why I was staying open. Even the ghoulish spectators who liked to hang out at crime scenes were avoiding me, and the local business folks had even stopped trickling in.

"These things seem to happen in spurts. I'm trying not to dwell on it, but what can you do? Tell me, how goes the art world?" I asked her, happy to see a familiar face. Annabeth and I had gone to high school together. She'd gotten her college degree in graphic design, but she was a true artist at heart in about every medium imaginable. While I was struggling to make ends meet on a daily basis, I had heard that Annabeth was doing quite well for herself in the high-flying art world.

"I'm keeping busy," she said, clearly trying to downplay her success in deference to my obvious lack of it. "I'd love an apple-stuffed donut and a cup of coffee," she added as she sat at the bar.

After I filled her order and delivered it, I said, "Annabeth, we've been friends a long time. You don't have to lie to me about your success to spare my feelings. Come on. Let me live a little vicariously through you. Talk to me!"

"Are you sure?" she asked. "The truth is, I've got some news I've been dying to tell somebody."

I grabbed a cup of coffee for myself and joined her. "Then I'm your gal. I'd love to hear all about it."

"Well, a certain high-tech company out west has asked me to submit some designs for a complete logo redesign. If you can believe it, they saw some of my work online and reached out to *me*. After they spotted a new logo I designed for a small espresso shop in New York, they checked out my website. You're not going to believe it, but what ultimately sold them wasn't so much my logo design work as it was the artwork I post there."

"Why shouldn't they be impressed? You're wonderfully talented. Wow, you're moving in completely different circles than the rest of us are these days," I said, truly happy for my friend. She deserved every bit of success she'd gotten with her graphic design and art career, and I was happy to know that she still enjoyed painting as well.

"Honestly, I think persistence is a lot more important than talent. I like to think that I've taken a tiny bit of ability and squeezed every last drop out of it I could. You remember more than anybody after college how hard I struggled finding clients for my design services or my art."

"Hey, you even painted my window for free donuts. I'm not about to forget that," I said with a grin. "If you want to barter for free donuts again, I'm always interested."

"Don't tease me, I might just take you up on your offer." She looked around the dining area and asked, "How would you feel about some new artwork for the shop?"

"I'd love it if it's from you," I said. Annabeth really did my heart and spirit good. She had one of those personalities you couldn't help but enjoy being around, and she seemed to make the world around her just a little brighter whenever she was in it.

"Don't worry so much, Suzanne. Whatever is going on in

your life right now won't last forever. You'll turn things around. I have all of the faith in the world in you."

"I'm glad that at least one of us does," I said, doing my best to smile. Things were a little rough at the moment on just about every front, but I knew in my heart that she was right. I'd gone through down times before, and things always seemed to work themselves out, though sometimes it had taken a hearty push from my husband, my family, and my friends.

As Annabeth tried to pay me for her donut and coffee, I pushed the money back toward her. "Consider it a down payment on my future artwork," I said with a grin. Even if it never materialized, her presence was well worth the price of a donut and coffee.

"Now I've *got* to do it," she said, smiling brightly as she headed out the door. "See you later."

"Bye," I said as I cleared away the dirty dishes. Since I had a moment, I put them in a bin and carried it into the kitchen. I supposed that was one plus that came from not being very busy. I didn't have all that many dishes to do.

But what was I going to do with my alarming surplus of donuts? I needed to do something other than throw them out with the trash. I decided that if folks weren't going to come to the donut shop, I was going to take my donut shop to them. I had my cart stored in back so I could give it a new paint job, but it was in perfectly fine shape for what I needed. Giving it a quick clean, I wheeled it around the building and parked it in front. In the past I'd used the cart for fairs and carnivals and such when I sold donuts away from the shop, but I was going to go mobile at home in April Springs! The worst that could happen was nothing, and I'd already been experiencing that. After I loaded up the cart, I had just a little over a dozen donuts left that wouldn't fit. I'd figure out what to do with them later, but for now it was time to make my way down the sidewalk toward city hall and see if I couldn't give away the treats I was going to have to throw out anyway and perhaps generate a little goodwill with my fellow residents along the way.

"How much are they?" Seth Lancaster asked as he studied my fully laden cart. He had been sitting on a bench near the town clock, but instead of getting up and coming to me, he had the nerve to wave me over to where he was sitting. Seth was a grumpy old man by nature, but lately he'd softened a bit. Not completely, but at least he'd managed to take some of his rough edges off.

"They're free. One per customer," I added, knowing full well that Seth might try to take advantage of my generosity.

"Got any pumpkin?" he asked as he studied my offerings keenly.

"No, sorry. It's not pumpkin donut season in the middle of summer," I told him.

"Humph," he said. "Coffee?"

I was getting exasperated with this man, but then I decided to smile instead. After all, I was trying to do a good thing here, and I wasn't going to let him spoil my intentions. "Nope. Not a drop," I said, my grin widening.

"Well, you don't have to be so happy about it," he grumbled.

"Seth, if you don't want a free donut, I understand. I'm sure someone else will."

I started to wheel the cart away, whistling like a fool as I did.

Wow, I hadn't realized Seth could move that quickly. He leapt from the bench and rushed toward me, awfully spry for a man his age. "Take it easy, Suzanne. I never said I didn't want one." After a moment's more thought, he said, "They all look good. Tell me something. What's your favorite?" Was he actually smiling as he said that last bit? I must have been seeing things. I knew that Seth had a softer side, but he so rarely showed it that it was almost impossible to recognize when it appeared.

"It's kind of hard to say. Answer me this. Which is your favorite grandchild?" I asked him. Seth had a soft spot for his four grandkids, and the entire town marveled at it.

"Emily," he said with a grin, "but if you tell anybody I said it, I'll deny it till I'm blue in the face."

"My lips are sealed," I said with an answering smile.

"Hang on a second. Maybe it's Noah," he amended. "When that boy laughs, his entire body shakes."

"Noah it is, then," I said.

"Then again, Hannah has an odd way of looking at the world that matches mine exactly. You want to know something? Patty is the hardest worker I've ever known in my life, and she *never* complains. Okay, you got me. I love them all equally, just for different reasons."

It had been an illuminating set of responses to a flippant question, but I was really glad that I'd asked it. Grabbing a bag from under the cart, I picked out five donuts and handed the bulging bag to him.

"I thought it was one per customer," he said.

"It is. Why don't you share these with your grandchildren?"

He grinned at me again. "Their parents are going to kill me when they find out I'm bringing donuts. This is perfect."

I could swear the man was almost skipping as he hurried down the street to share my goodies with his grandkids.

I was still smiling about it when I spotted George Morris walking toward me.

One look at his face told me that things were not going any better for our mayor than they had the last time I'd seen him.

"What's up, Mr. Mayor," I said as I tried to put on a smile, hoping that it would somehow be infectious. "Care for a free donut?"

"Sure. Why not?" he asked with a shrug as he selected a sour cream donut, one of my favorites as well. "Has it come to that? You have to give them away now because of me?"

"You didn't kill Cassandra," I said, scolding him lightly, "and you need to quit moping around town feeling sorry for yourself. The way that you're acting, you even look guilty to me, and I *know* you didn't do it."

"How can you be sure?" he asked, the defeat clear in his voice.

"George, you *never* would have pushed a giant donut onto her," I said. "Frankly, you lack the imagination. No offense intended," I said with a smile. George was my crustiest friend. We'd always had a relationship where we could be brutally honest with each other to the point where other people listening in thought we were being downright mean. They just didn't understand the dynamic George and I shared.

"None taken," he replied with the hint of a smile cracking through. "What am I going to do, Suzanne? It's killing me that I can't investigate this myself, but I believe the chief. He'll lock me up if he catches me meddling."

"Maybe so, but you can help me in my investigation. I know you've been thinking about who might have killed Cassandra. Do you have a list for me?"

"Yeah, it's true that I've been giving it some thought," George said. "As a matter of fact, I was going to take this over to Chief Grant."

"Mind if I have a look at it first?" I asked. "The chief's kind of tied up at the moment, anyway."

George handed the sheet of paper over, and after reading the list of names, I took a photo of it with my phone before I handed it back to him.

"What's going on that's keeping the police chief so busy, Suzanne?"

"He's trying to track down Marybeth Jenkins," I said, not realizing that George probably didn't know about her crush on him and her efforts to protect him. It seemed as though I was spilling all kinds of Marybeth's secrets lately, but it was too late to go back now. Besides, the mayor had a right to know.

"Why on earth would he want to speak with her?"

"It turns out that she had an argument with Cassandra yesterday evening," I said.

"Really? What about?"

"You," I said, watching his expression.

He was clearly baffled and clueless about her feelings for him. "Me? Why?"

"George, she's had a crush on you for years, and she didn't like the way Cassandra had been treating you. She threatened her, by her own admission, and now Cassandra is dead. When I urged her to tell the chief what happened, she chose to drive off instead, and he's out looking for her even as we speak."

"Marybeth? She never said a word to me," George said, shaking his head.

"She was too shy," I told him.

"Not too shy to confront Cassandra, though," George said with a bit of uncertainty in his voice. "I don't know what to make of all that. It's completely caught me off guard."

"Well, you're probably the *only* one in town who didn't realize it," I said. "Tell me about that list of names you wrote down." When he didn't respond immediately, I pushed him a little harder. "George, you need to focus on this. It's important."

"You're right," George said after taking another bite of his donut. "This list might not be complete, but it's certainly a good place to start."

I pulled it up on my phone to be sure that I'd be able to read it later, and I started at the top of the list and began to work my way down.

"Talk to me," I said.

"I'm not sure how good it is. I didn't even know about Marybeth," George answered, still clearly shaken by my revelation.

"That's why you're not in this alone," I said. "Who exactly is Heather Lindquist?"

"Her brother was murdered by Thomas Allan Smythe in Union Square three years ago," George said.

"I remember the case," I said, "but what does that have to do with Cassandra?"

"She got the killer off scot-free, even though it was obvious to everyone that he'd done it. Having that confession thrown out was a travesty of justice, and it shouldn't have come as a surprise to anyone that the moment Smythe was out, he killed someone else almost immediately. Heather has threatened Cassandra on more than one occasion, and she's been stalking her around town lately."

"George, are you telling me that the *chief* doesn't even know what's been happening?" I asked. It was hard to imagine that Cassandra, or even the mayor, hadn't gone to the chief of police if there had been any kind of serious threat against her.

"I tried to talk her into it, but she wouldn't let me tell him. She thought Heather was harmless, but I always worried about her."

"Okay," I said. "We'll be sure to check her out. How about this Bernie Nance?"

"He's one of the bad ones, Suzanne, another one of Cassandra's clients," George acknowledged.

"Did he get away with murder, too?" I asked. I knew that defense attorneys were a necessary part of our legal system, but I didn't know how anyone could stomach dealing with so many people who had clearly committed some pretty heinous acts. It must be a depressing way to live your life, but what did I know? I was sure there was probably real satisfaction making sure that innocent people were exonerated, but how must you feel after securing the release of someone clearly guilty of their accused crime? I personally wasn't meant for such high stakes. It was one of the reasons no one's life or death ever ended up in my hands. The worst my donuts could do was make folks fat, and that was just if they overindulged in my treats over a very long period of time. Then again, I'd been accused of being a killer before, and if I'd ever gone to trial, I would have wanted someone with Cassandra's skill set defending me.

"Suzanne? Did I lose you?" George asked.

"No, I was just trying to understand why Cassandra did what she did, or more importantly, how she managed to live with the consequences of her successes, as well as her failures."

"She never had any trouble sleeping at night if that's what you're asking. As a cop, once and always, I couldn't understand how she could put so much time and energy undoing what we lived for, but the fact is, she was a necessary evil. The thing is, with Cassandra, it was all about winning. She was driven like nobody else I've ever known, and that made her some very real enemies."

"Clearly," I said. "Tell me about Bernie."

"He still swears that he was innocent, a man in the wrong place at the wrong time, but Cassandra couldn't get him out of a murder conviction. It was overturned on appeal, but not before he'd spent seven years in prison. The moment he got out, he moved to Maple Hollow, and he's been trying to get into Cassandra's head ever since."

"What happened originally?" I asked.

"He was convicted of intentionally knocking a car jack out from a muscle car his brother was working on during an argument they were having. It crushed the man to death. A witness said she heard the argument and saw the whole thing, and Cassandra couldn't shake her testimony. It turned out that she had been lying, high as a kite on drugs at the time. Only after she got clean and sober did she recant her testimony, and Bernie was finally released."

"I can understand him being resentful about the eyewitness," I said. "So why isn't he going after her?"

"As a matter of fact, she died last week," George said soberly. "I just heard about it."

"What happened?" I asked, feeling a knot in the pit of my stomach.

"Somebody shoved her in front of a bus," George said. "They have no idea who did it."

"Do you think it might have been Bernie?" I asked him. I couldn't imagine how someone could do such a thing, but then again, I hadn't been wrongfully imprisoned for seven years, either.

"I'm not willing to discount it," George said. "Before he was arrested for killing his brother, he had a history of assault and battery. The man has a nasty streak a mile wide."

"Okay, we'll track him down, too. Is there anybody else?" I asked as I glanced back at the list, suddenly feeling a little depressed despite the beauty of the day. Murder investigations did that to me, especially when I started investigating possible suspects. It was alarming how many folks had a reason to want to see someone else dead. The next name on the list caught me by surprise. "Mary Paris? Seriously? Why would a housekeeper want to kill Cassandra?"

"It all started as a misunderstanding, but things escalated pretty quickly," George said. "Mary was cleaning Cassandra's condo, and Cassandra's diamond pin in the shape of a fountain pen went missing right afterwards. Cassandra was positive that Mary stole it, which she denied. Not only did Cassandra fire her, but she threatened to have her arrested if it didn't turn up. She and Mary had a pretty bad argument two nights ago, and Cassandra gave her a deadline to return the pin, or she was going to jail." George added, "The deadline expired at midnight last night."

I couldn't imagine Mary killing anyone. A tall, thin woman, she was severe at times, very thorough at what she did, and I knew firsthand that she took her reputation extremely seriously. I remembered a time when she'd allowed me to search a victim's place, making me work the entire time I was there. I knew that she could be hard to deal with at times, but could she commit murder? "Do you honestly think she might have done it?"

"You should have seen her, Suzanne. I didn't know she had it in her, but Cassandra had a way of pushing people beyond what they could take. It didn't help that Mary had just been dumped by her boyfriend, so she was already on edge anyway, and Cassandra knew it. My late girlfriend never managed to leave her tactics of intimidation in the courtroom. She had a habit of upsetting a great many people, and she always seemed to leave quite a wake in her path wherever she went."

"I can't imagine that Mary actually stole the pin, no matter how fragile she might have been," I said.

"The fact is that it will probably turn up once I clean out Cassandra's place. The chief's released it, and I'm set to ship what's important to her sister in Seattle. That's where the body's going," George said, choking up. "I don't know how I'm going to face it."

"You shouldn't have to," I said. "Grace and I will do it for you."

George looked at me askance. "Are you offering to do it to help me avoid an unpleasant situation, or are you going there to try to track down her killer?"

"Can't it be a little bit of both?" I asked him. "You asked me to help, remember? So let me do this."

"I would appreciate that very much," George said. He reached into his pocket and pulled out a key. "Here you go. Thanks for digging into this case, Suzanne."

"You're very welcome," I said. "Now you should probably take that list of yours to the police chief. Who knows? He might even be back by now."

George frowned. "Are you sure you don't want a crack at those names first yourself?"

I'd been tempted to suggest that very thing myself, but then I'd realized that it might not hurt to have Chief Grant talk to our list of suspects first. I knew that I was giving up the element of surprise, but I thought that hardly mattered in the cases of Heather Lindquist and Bernie Nance. Once they learned of Cassandra's murder, they *had* to know that they'd be questioned. Marybeth was already on the run, so that just left Mary Paris. She might have to be near the top of our list, but honestly, searching Cassandra's place had to be our number one priority. I knew from past experience that there was no substitute for digging into a person's life by going through the things they'd inadvertently left behind.

"Sure, I wouldn't mind the first crack at them, but honestly, the chief needs to see what you've got to say. Your reputation is on the line here, George. If you can help Chief Grant solve the case without us, no one would be happier than I would be."

"You two are still going to look into it though, right?" he asked, clearly hoping that I wasn't having second thoughts.

"Absolutely. I don't see what it could hurt if Grace and I poke around and see what we can find." I looked at the cart, still carrying quite a few more donuts than I was happy with. "Let me wheel this back to the shop, and I'll start shutting down for the day."

"If you want to unload the rest of it, follow me into city hall. I'll make an announcement on the intercom on my way to see the chief, and unless I miss my guess, those buzzards will clean you out in a flash."

"Thanks, but I don't want you to use your influence to help me," I answered.

"Nonsense. They'll all think I'm a hero for getting them free donuts," he said, managing the hint of a smile.

The mayor was right. Within four minutes of his making the announcement, my cart was empty.

I headed back to Donut Hearts to clean up for the day and go in search of Grace to see if she'd be able to help me on this case.

When I got near the shop, I saw that she'd saved me the trouble.

My best friend was standing in front of Donut Hearts, staring impatiently at the locked door as she pulled out her cell phone.

It didn't even surprise me when mine rang an instant later.

I chose not to answer it as I snuck up behind her. "You called?" I asked, clearly catching her off guard.

"There you are," Grace said as she put her phone back in her purse. "Where have you been?"

"Handing out free donuts," I said as I unlocked the door and we went inside.

"Has it come to that, Suzanne? Are things really that bad?" she asked.

"I'm just trying to be proactive like you advised me to be," I replied.

"Okay, but the object is to *make* money, not give your goods away for free," she reminded me.

"Don't worry about me. There's method to my madness," I

said as I pushed the cart to one side and locked the door behind us. "Are you up for a little sleuthing?"

"I wish I could," she said, looking a little disappointed that she had to refuse my request. That made two of us. "That's why I stopped by. My new boss has volunteered my services someplace else. Apparently they have a management team in dire need of a shakeup, though why she thought of me as the one to do it is hard to imagine." After a moment, she added, "You know, maybe it's not such a bad thing that I leave town for a few weeks at that."

"Wow, you're sure going to a lot of trouble not to help me with my anniversary party and my investigation into who killed Cassandra Lane," I said with a smile, trying to lighten my friend's obvious load.

"It's not that, and you know it. I figured George would rope you into doing it. I'm just sorry I can't help you. If I could get out of this trip, I'd honestly try, but I wasn't really given an option. I hate leaving you in the lurch with so many things up in the air, but honestly, after the way Stephen and I left things last night, I've got a feeling we could both use a break from each other."

"Was it really all that bad?" I asked her.

"He didn't say anything to you about it, did he?"

"No, not about you, but then again, he knows I try to stay away from meddling in your relationship." I looked at Grace and found her grinning at me.

"Really? You don't honestly believe that, do you?"

I had to laugh. "At least I'm trying. Don't I at least get credit for that?"

"I suppose so," she said. "Things are so much more complicated dating as an adult, aren't they?"

"Funny, but I don't remember dating in high school or

college being much easier, either," I reminded her. "I think it's hard to do at any age."

"And yet you've gotten at least two men to marry you, and I still haven't gotten a nibble."

"Need I remind you how disastrous my first marriage was?" I asked.

"Maybe, but at least you got a donut shop out of the deal," she replied. "Anyway, I'd better be going. I've got a twelve-hour drive ahead of me. When they give you a company car, they actually have the nerve to expect you to use it on the company's behalf."

"What nerve," I said with a smile as I hugged her. "I'll miss you, and not just for your sleuthing abilities."

"Will you be able to get someone else to help you? Obviously George won't work, but you could always ask your mother."

"That's where I'm going as soon as I finish cleaning up. Don't worry about me. Call me when you stop for the night, okay? I worry about you."

"What makes you think I won't just drive straight through?" she asked.

"If there's a chance to stay in a nice place along the way and spoil yourself, I can't imagine you passing up the opportunity."

That made her laugh again. "How well you know me." After a moment's pause, she said, "Be careful, Suzanne. If someone is crazy enough to murder Cassandra with a giant donut, they are probably capable of anything."

"I'll watch my back," I promised her.

After Grace was gone, I locked the door behind her and set about my closing tasks. The deposit wasn't even large enough to bother with. I put the money in the safe and went about the routine of doing a pile of dishes so I'd be ready to face tomorrow.

Hopefully it would produce better results than the day I'd just gone through had.

If I had any luck at all, I'd do better at sleuthing than peddling donuts anyway, but only time would tell.

CHAPTER 9

INSTEAD OF GOING BACK TO my empty cottage, I decided to head straight to Momma's to see if she felt like pitching in on another investigation. We'd worked surprisingly well together in the past on a few occasions, and while Jake and Grace were my first choices, Momma was definitely a viable option. After that, George was a solid partner, and I'd even worked on a few things with my stepfather, Phillip, the former police chief for April Springs. It was funny, but I found that I liked him a lot better once he wasn't in charge of things.

I had a feeling he felt the same way about me.

I was about to knock on their door when Phillip opened it before I could finish my task. He had lost a great deal of weight when he'd been courting my mother, but a little of it had come back since, though not nearly as much as it had once been. "Hey, Suzanne. I was just about to head over to the donut shop."

"I have a few extras in the back of my Jeep," I volunteered. "You're welcome to whatever I've still got."

"Really? Are there any sour cream cake donuts, by any chance?"

"I think there's one there. Let's go check." As we walked back to the Jeep, I asked, "Is that really why you were coming by to see me?"

"No, I have a message for you from your mother. She's going out of town for a few days, and she wanted me to tell you not to worry if you didn't hear from her."

"Why didn't she call me herself?" I asked him. It wasn't like Momma not to keep me up to speed on her whereabouts.

"She tried, but for some reason she couldn't get you. Did you have your cell phone off this morning, by any chance?"

I suddenly remembered that I'd turned it off for a bit so I could concentrate on making donuts, and then I'd forgotten to turn it back on until later. My goodness, the older I got, the more forgetful I seemed to be. If I was already losing my mind in my thirties, I was in for some serious trouble down the road. "I left it on the counter when I took my cart over to city hall," I admitted. "Where is she going?"

"She's got some kind of real estate opportunity in Howling Rock," he said, naming a resort town about an hour from us, straight up into the Blue Ridge Mountains and not far from the Parkway. The once-sleepy town was known for its quaint charm but also for the loads of tourists who permeated the place like blackflies in summer.

"I didn't think she was a big fan of the place," I said.

"I don't either, but one of her old rivals is offering to cut her in on a deal that seems too good to be true, so she couldn't pass it up."

"She always told me that if it seems too good to be true, it probably is," I said with a smile.

"I know. I teased her about that very expression, but she just can't bring herself not to at least check it out."

"I'm a bit surprised you didn't go with her," I said as I found the donut Phillip had requested. "Sorry, but I don't have any napkins with me."

"That's okay. I can just lick my fingers when I'm finished," he said with a smile. "As to going with her, I love the mountains, but I got the impression that I would just be a distraction she didn't need. Honestly, I was happy to stay here. The truth is that there was another reason she didn't want me to go," he added a little ominously.

"You two aren't having problems, are you?" I asked him. I'd been against their relationship from the start, but over time, Phillip Martin had won me over. It had been clear that he dearly loved my mother and had for most of his life, and much to my surprise, she returned it in full.

"No, on the contrary, we've never been stronger. As a matter of fact, I'm sticking around for you."

That shocked me. "Me? I'm fine. Why would you and Momma think I needed anyone to watch out for me?"

"With George in trouble and Jake gone, she was worried that Grace wouldn't be enough of a support system for you. Suzanne, we're family. I know I'm just your mother's husband, but you have to know that you matter to me." It was the most honest, emotional thing the man had ever said to me.

"I really appreciate that, Phillip. You matter to me, too." He might not have been my first choice as an ally, and in fact, the former police chief was the last one on my list of potential partners in my investigation, but at least he was *on* the list somewhere, and that was all that counted. "Grace had to leave town suddenly," I admitted, "and George has been forbidden to go anywhere near this investigation. Would you have any interest in helping me dig into Cassandra Lane's murder?"

"I suppose that depends," he said, his lips suddenly pursed together.

"On what?"

"Do I get any more donuts?" he asked me with a hearty grin.

"I've only got a dozen left, but you're entitled to every last one of them," I offered, returning his smile with one of my own.

"Then I'm in," he said. "Do you have a list of suspects, or are we starting from square one?"

"I do have a list of names, but there's something even more

pressing. George has asked me to clean out Cassandra's place," I replied as I dangled her house key in the air. "Care to join me?"

"Sure," he said with a shrug. "And here I thought I'd be able to be a slob batching it with your mother gone."

"You can do whatever you want to here," I said, "but we need to look for clues at Cassandra's and sort through her things while we're doing it. George is sending anything valuable or sentimental to her sister, and the rest we're donating to charity. It's for a good cause, and it should save our friend some heartache having to do it himself."

"I'm all in, then," Phillip said. "Let me grab a few trash bags and boxes from the garage, and we can go. Should we take my truck? I'm not sure how much we'd be able to get in that Jeep of yours."

"Sure, why not?" I asked.

"While we're driving over there, you can catch me up on what I've missed so far."

It appeared that I'd gotten a sleuthing partner after all, just not one that I had expected. Still, Phillip had been a good police chief when he'd served April Springs, and if anything, his mind had grown sharper since retiring. He'd devoted his spare time digging into old cold cases, and he'd had some success where those before him had failed. All in all, we should make a pretty good team investigating Cassandra's murder. I just hoped that Phillip and I solved it, and quickly, before George's reputation was beyond repair.

It always felt odd being in a place that had belonged to someone who had just died, whether they passed away on the premises or not. I didn't think it showed, though.

"Is there something wrong, Suzanne?" Phillip asked me as I hesitated at the door.

"No, I'm all right," I said, fighting down my feelings as I tried to approach this as methodically as I could. "Would you like the kitchen or the bedroom?" I asked as I looked around the stylish though rather small condominium apartment. As expected, Cassandra's tastes were impeccable, which was obvious from the moment we'd walked through the front door. She'd managed to take a decent space and turn it into something any designer could be proud of. It was all very neat as well, with everything having its place, and I felt a little envious for the late woman's discipline.

"If it's all the same to you, I'll start out here." I figured the former police chief made his choice because he didn't want to deal with Cassandra's clothing, most specifically, her bras and panties. It amazed me how simple undergarments could befuzzle the most toughened man sometimes.

"No worries," I said as I grabbed a bag and a box. "I'll take the bedroom."

The bed was made, everything was in its place, and the closet seemed to be perfectly organized. Again, it looked ready for a photo shoot. At first I couldn't figure out what was bothering me about it. After all, no one could have asked for a neater, more stylish and tidy place to live. And then I realized what it was.

The entire apartment was *too* immaculate, *too* impersonal. There wasn't a photo, a memento, not even a keepsake of any kind within sight. Was this a woman or a robot, for goodness sake? As expected, as I went through the dresser drawers, I found that everything was folded neatly and placed just so. She certainly had an orderly mind, as well as living habits. It made the search easy, if uneventful. I soon had the first donation bag full, without a single item in the KEEP box I'd brought in with me. I went out into the living room to grab another bag and found Phillip methodically going through each box of food from the pantry, spilling the contents into a trash can as he went.

"I need another bag," I said, grabbing one and then hesitating to watch him work. "Are you looking for anything in particular?"

"You'd be amazed at what I've found in cereal boxes over the years," he said with a shrug.

"For example? I mean besides the expected breakfast food contents."

"Let's see. I've found handguns, ammunition, stolen jewelry, enough cash to finance a trip to Hawaii, and more than one clue in solving a crime," he said.

"Really? That's interesting. You really should write a book," I suggested.

He grinned at me ruefully. "I'll have to pass on that idea. I tried to once. It was as dull as dishwater. I don't know how these writers do it. They somehow manage to make the most mundane events sound interesting. They make it look easy, too."

"It's been my experience in the past that the easier a thing looks, the harder it is to master to make it look effortless," I said. "Have you discovered anything yet?"

"Just that she had her cereals alphabetized in the pantry. The woman may have been a lot of things, but haphazard was certainly not on the list. How about you?"

"I haven't found anything personal yet, and I'm nearly through with her drawers."

"Did she really have that much underwear?" he asked tentatively. "You've taken all that time on just that?"

I had to laugh. "Not her underwear, I'm talking about the entire chest of drawers containing her clothes, both under – and outer garments," I said.

"Yeah. Sure," he said, his face reddening slightly. "Call me if you find anything."

"You, too," I said as I headed back into the bedroom to resume my search.

The dresser was a total wash, and I was starting to give up on the closet as well when I noticed a heavy cardboard box pushed to one side. On the top, in neat lettering, it said simply "Personal".

This I had to see. Perhaps Cassandra had a sentimental bone in her body after all.

I was glad George hadn't been the one to search her apartment. Apparently Cassandra kept souvenirs of past and current loves, some of them dating well before she'd ever met our mayor. That was fair enough. The woman had been entitled to a life of her own before she came into George's, and if she chose to hang on to a few keepsakes, that had certainly been her business. I carefully dumped them out onto the bed and put them back in reverse order so everything would be as I had first discovered it. The box went all the way back to her teenage years, and it seemed to me as though she'd only kept one item from each of her past paramours, judging by the diversity of the tokens she'd hung onto. When I got near the end of my search, which was also near the top of her keepsakes, I found a flyer from the previous Halloween Fright Week, an event which she'd helped George run. All in all, there was nothing of interest there, nothing that would help our investigation, at any rate.

At least that's what I thought until I got to the very last item in the box. Did that mean that this had been added *while* she'd been dating George? It was a receipt from a place called the Claremont Inn in Union Square. If she'd gone there to be with George, why had she kept the Fright Week flyer as well? For that matter, why go to a hotel at all if they were both living in April Springs, less than a thirty-minute drive away? I had always thought of it as a nice, respectable midlevel hotel, a place to stay while traveling for business, not some seedy motel designed for an illicit tryst. I'd need to look into that further, especially since the receipt was dated from just two days before.

I was about to take it in to show my partner in crime after taking a quick picture of it with my cell phone when I heard Phillip exclaim from the other room.

What on earth was that all about?

CHAPTER 10

"WHAT IS IT? WHAT DID you find?" I asked as I rushed into the living room.

Phillip was grinning at me as he held a diamond pin aloft. The pin, which had to be the one Cassandra had accused Mary Paris of stealing, was in the shape of a fountain pen, and he had already put it into a small evidence bag, clearly something he'd done upon retrieving it.

"Where was it?"

"Under the couch cushion," Phillip said triumphantly. "I had to really dig down to find it, so it doesn't surprise me that Cassandra must have missed it in her earlier searches."

"This vindicates Mary, at least," I said.

"Maybe of theft, but not of murder," Phillip said softly as he shook the bag. "You said it yourself. Cassandra accused her openly of stealing from her, and the damage to Mary's reputation could have been insurmountable."

"Does that mean that we have to turn it over to the police chief?" I asked.

"Well, we can't exactly give it to Cassandra's sister." He must have spotted the receipt in my hand. "What's that?"

I'd nearly forgotten about it myself. "Evidently Cassandra kept a memento from every one of her love affairs, but just a single item."

"So, she and George went to a hotel in Union Square. What does that prove?"

"That's the problem. I don't think she went there with George," I said. "I also found a flyer from Fright Week. *That* had to be George's token." I waved the receipt in the air. "I don't know who this belongs to."

"Put it in here," he said as he produced another evidence bag.

"Do you go anywhere without those?" I asked as I did what he asked.

"Not when I'm working on something," Phillip admitted. "Hey, we're making some real progress here, aren't we?"

"Slowly but surely," I said. "I'm going to leave this with you and finish up in her bedroom. After that, I'll tackle her office, if that's okay with you."

"Go ahead and be my guest. I've got plenty left to do here."

"Would you mind helping me flip the bed over?" I asked him. "She might have put something under her mattress."

"I'd be happy to help," he said.

Unfortunately, there was nothing of note between the mattresses or under the bed, either.

Phillip went back to his assignment while I stayed in the bedroom, giving everything one last look before finishing up there.

As I moved into the office, I found myself hoping that we'd find something there a little more concrete than what we'd come up with so far. As things stood, the pile to send on to Cassandra's sister was rather stark, as well as our collected clues.

Everybody was always talking about going paperless, but Cassandra was clearly a proponent of the concept. There was a mini-scanner by her computer and a shredder beside her desk. I turned her computer on, but it was no surprise when I realized that it was password protected. It would take someone with more than my minimal computer skills to bypass that, so I moved the laptop to one side and began searching through the desk drawers, looking for some kind of hint. I knew that Cassandra worked out of her home office since she'd moved to town, so this was all that I was going to be able to look through.

Unfortunately, there wasn't much there.

I was about to give up when I noticed that above the top drawer of her desk, there was a narrow shelf that could be pulled out to extend the working surface.

I wasn't really expecting to find anything there, but gladly, I was wrong.

Stuck to the thin top was a half sheet of paper carefully taped around its edges. As I glanced over what was written on it, I found a host of names that instantly caught my eye.

Heather Lindquist was listed, as well as Bernie Nance. Mary Paris was on it, too, as well as a few other names I didn't recognize, Shelly Hastings and Richard Beacon, but there was one name there that I'd hoped wouldn't make the list.

George Morris.

Worse yet, at the top of the note, there was a carefully handwritten line that put a chill all the way through me.

Who Would Want To See Me Come To Harm?

Why had the attorney made the list in the first place? Had there been a threat against her life that we weren't aware of? If so, the killer might have gone through with it and ended Cassandra Lane's life.

Only now it was up to us to find the answer to that question. Who, indeed.

"Phillip, I found something else you need to see," I said.

"What is it?" he asked, eager to see what I'd come up with.

"It's taped to Cassandra's desk, and I didn't want to take a chance on tearing it before I showed it to you." That was certainly true enough, but thankfully I'd been able to take a photo of it as well. What did people do before their telephones had cameras? I wasn't the biggest fan of every advance in technology ever made, but I knew that the modern cell phone, along with all it could do, was a lifesaver when I was working on a case.

"I'll grab a knife," Phillip said, and he followed me into the office.

"Did you get a photo of this first?" my stepfather asked me.

"What makes you ask that?" I deflected.

He smiled gently. "Suzanne, I've known you a long time. Frankly, I'd be disappointed in you if you hadn't."

"No worries there, then. I've got it covered," I said, answering his grin with one of my own.

"Good." Taking the knife, he carefully cut the tape, freeing the notepaper rather elegantly. After placing it in yet another evidence bag, he turned to me. "To tell you the truth, I wish George's name wasn't on this list."

"Me, too, but we can't just erase it or cut it out," I answered.

The former police chief looked shocked that I'd even suggested it. "Suzanne, you're kidding, right? You know that we can't tamper with what might be evidence, even to save our friend."

"I said we couldn't do it," I argued, though half-heartedly.

Phillip grabbed his cell phone, and at first I thought it was to take a photo himself, but then I saw him dialing a number. "Do I even have to ask you who you're calling?"

"The chief needs to see all of this," Phillip said.

"Agreed," I said as I put my hand on his, stopping him for at least a moment. "But does it have to be this second? Can't we finish searching the apartment first?"

"I suppose it can wait until then," he said.

"After all, the chief must have given this place a pretty quick look himself, even if he didn't find anything."

"Give him a break. He's got a lot on his plate at the moment.

I'm sure he assigned one of his people to the job." Phillip glanced at his wristwatch, and then he frowned. "We can wait ten minutes, but then I'm calling Chief Grant. Sorry, but it's the most I can give you."

"Ten minutes it is, then," I said, not wanting to argue with him about it. Besides, I was nearly finished with my search anyway.

Unfortunately, the delay did me no good. Neither Phillip nor I found anything else of interest by the time we'd finished our mutual searches. It had been worth a shot, though.

"Go ahead. Make the call," I told my stepfather as I looked at the three things we'd found.

At first glance it didn't look like all that much, but I knew that any one of the items we found could turn out to be significant in the end.

I just didn't know how at the moment, but I was going to do my utmost to find out.

"I can't believe you're meddling into one of my murder investigations again," the chief told me the second he arrived at Cassandra's place. "Suzanne, how did you ever get it in your head that you're qualified to investigate a homicide?"

I was about to reply when Phillip surprised us both by speaking up first. "You need to take it easy there, Chief."

"You're actually *defending* her?" Chief Grant asked, clearly more than a little bit irritated with his former boss. "I remember you singing a different tune when she was meddling with one of *your* investigations, and now you're partnering up with her."

"I'd like to think that I can learn from my past mistakes," he said. "Suzanne brings something to the table that neither one of us does. She has insights into ordinary folks that we miss at times. I'm proud she called me," Phillip answered. He must have been able to tell that the chief was about to retort when he quickly added, "Don't forget, you released this apartment, and we're doing George a favor. What should we have done when we stumbled upon a few clues that your folks missed? Disregard them completely and just pretend nothing happened?"

"No, of course not," he said. "As to my staff missing things, trust me, I'll be taking that up with them later. I can't be everywhere, blast it all. My job is hard enough without looking over everyone else's shoulder to make sure they are doing what they are supposed to be doing. Darby was supposed to handle this, and he clearly blew it. He and I are going to have ourselves a serious little chat the next time I see him."

"You need to trust your people," the former chief said gently. "Anyone can make a mistake or miss something. None of us is perfect."

Wow, this man standing beside me really had changed since his time as our chief of police. Sometimes it was hard for me to believe, but I knew that my mother had influenced him since they'd been together, and as far as I was concerned, nearly every change he'd made had been for the better.

"Yes, of course, you're right," the chief said, finally lowering his voice and easing his tone. He turned to me after a moment and added, "Sorry about my little snit, Suzanne. I've got a lot going on at the moment, not that I have to tell you that."

"If you're talking about Grace, she hasn't told me anything about what's been going on between the two of you," I admitted, as much as it pained me to say.

Chief Grant looked honestly stunned by that. "Seriously? She hasn't even talked about it to *you*?"

"Not really," I said. "Maybe she'll want to discuss it when she gets back to April Springs."

"She's *gone?*" Stephen Grant asked. For that instant, he sounded nothing like the chief of police but more like a boyfriend who was completely in the dark about his significant other's situation.

"Call her, Stephen," I prodded him. "You can't just leave things the way they are right now."

The current chief of police took all of that in, and after a moment, he seemed to try to clear it from his mind. "I should have never brought it up in the first place." After running a hand through his hair, he continued, "Okay, let's see what you've found."

Phillip nodded as he brought the items out one at a time. "We found this under the couch," he said as he held the diamond pen pin in the air.

"So, Mary Paris didn't take it after all," the chief said.

"No, but as Phillip pointed out to me, she still had motive enough to kill Cassandra for trying to ruin her good name. It's even worse now that we know that it was without cause," I said.

"True enough. That woman is as fierce as a mother bear protecting her cubs when it comes to her reputation. Still, I'm glad this has been found. We can stop searching for it."

"Have you really been looking for it?" I asked.

After the chief nodded, he said, "Not only might it be an important part of the case, but Cassandra's sister has been howling about it. Evidently it's not only valuable, but it's some kind of family heirloom. I won't be able to release it right away, but at least we know where it is now. What else do you two have for me?" he asked as he pocketed the pin.

Phillip looked at me. "It's your turn, Suzanne. You're the one who found the next two items."

"You were here with me, though," I said, not wanting to take all of the credit.

"I don't care who shows me, let's just see what you've got," the chief said a little impatiently.

"Okay. First of all, there's this," I said, pulling out the box of mementos Cassandra kept in her closet. Without any background information, it might be more difficult for the chief to see why the receipt I'd found could be important. "It appears that Cassandra kept one item from every relationship she had," I said as I tapped the box. "On the very top was this," I added as I nodded to Phillip to present the receipt in question.

He took it and then almost immediately dismissed it. "So she had a tryst with George in Union Square. I don't see what the big deal is about that."

"There was a flyer for Fright Week that represented George, unless I miss my guess," I said. "The receipt must be for someone else."

"I'm not sure I follow your logic," the chief said. "Maybe she collects several things during a relationship and then, once it's over, she chooses the most significant item to keep."

"I hadn't thought of it that way," I admitted. Somehow it still felt wrong. "Would you at least *ask* George if that's true? If they spent that night together, it would ease my mind quite a bit."

"I'll check with him later," he said, putting the bagged receipt with the pin. "What else?"

"This is our big find," I said.

Phillip handed him the list, and the chief studied it for a moment before replying. "Who would want to see me come to harm? That's quite a question, isn't it?"

"Two of those names on the list aren't familiar to me," I said, "and I can't believe that she honestly suspected George of anything."

"And yet she put his name on her list," the chief said.

"What about Shelly Hastings and Richard Beacon?" Phillip

asked the chief. I would have had to glance at the note again to recall their names, but evidently my stepfather had a better memory than I did.

"You can forget Shelly Hastings right off the bat," the chief replied.

"Why is that?"

"She made my list as well," Chief Grant said. "I checked up on her, since she threatened to kill Cassandra when she lost her case several years ago. Ms. Hastings was released from prison ten days ago."

"So, that should make her a prime suspect," I said. What was the chief thinking, dismissing the woman so nonchalantly?

"It would, except for the fact that she's been locked up in Maple Hollow after trying to rob a convenience store there six days ago," he replied.

"What about Richard Beacon, then?"

"His name crossed my desk as well. He's actually got an ongoing civil case against Cassandra for failure to pay a bill from him, and he got pretty angry with her last week when she refused to give him another dime."

"What did he do for her?" I asked.

"He retiled a floor in her house or something before she put it on the market, and she claimed the job was botched from start to finish. He denied the accusation, and he took her to court. It was heard three days ago, and he lost, hands down. They had to yank him from Small Claims Court for going after Cassandra with his bare hands. Evidently the man is some sort of hothead."

"Surely he's a viable suspect," I said.

"As soon as we can track him down, we have some questions for him," the chief admitted. "I understand he's doing a job in Union Square at the moment, so he shouldn't be that hard to find."

"Speaking of tracking people down, have you had any luck finding Marybeth Jenkins?" I asked.

"No, not yet, but don't worry. We'll find her."

"How can you be so sure?" Phillip asked.

"You know how these things go. She'll turn up sooner or later."

"I hope you're right," I said, though I lacked his confidence that it would be as easy and as painless as he was making it sound. "Anyway, that's all we found. We've gone through the entire place. There's a big pile to donate but just a few personal objects to pass on to Cassandra's sister." Something suddenly occurred to me. "Did you have any luck getting past her password on her computer?"

"Did you try to get into it yourself?" the chief asked me, studying me a bit as he asked.

"Of course I did," I readily admitted. After all, there had been nothing wrong with me doing it, at least not as far as I was concerned.

"We managed to crack the code," he admitted with a smile. "The password was written on a sticky note stuck under the computer itself. I can't believe how lax people are about their security."

Cassandra had written her password, and she'd put it *under* her computer? Why had I not thought of lifting it up and checking myself? I felt a bit like an idiot for missing something that was clearly so obvious.

"Okay, we're going to go ahead and load my truck with all of this so we can donate everything," Phillip said.

"Why don't you just do me a favor and leave everything right where it is?" the chief suggested.

"You don't want us to go ahead and donate it?" I asked him.

"I want Darby to go through everything one more time before we do that," the chief said.

"Are you suggesting that we might have missed something?"

I asked, feeling a little indignant about the issue even being raised.

Before he could answer, Phillip smiled at me. "He's not questioning our thoroughness. The chief is going to try to teach one of his officers a lesson on the importance of being thorough." Phillip turned to Chief Grant and asked, "Isn't that right?"

"It's dead on the money," the current chief said. "Do you mind giving me your copy of the apartment key?"

"I'm happy to," I said as I handed it over to him. It really didn't matter to me anymore. I was certain that we'd gotten everything there was to find in Cassandra's apartment. Let the chief's deputy spin his wheels.

Phillip and I had other things to do.

After we left Cassandra's, Phillip asked, "Where to now?"

"I don't know about you, but I'd love to see Mary Paris's face when she finds out that pin has been recovered." After a moment, I asked, "Do you think the chief would be upset with us if we told her first?"

"He never said anything about us keeping it quiet," Phillip said with a smile. "It just makes sense that we'd go ahead and tell her ourselves, doesn't it? After all, I'm sure Mary will be relieved to know she's in the clear, at least about the theft."

"It might be interesting to see how she reacts to the news, especially if she was the one who pushed that donut on top of Cassandra."

"I still can't believe someone chose that as a murder weapon. It took some pretty serious nerve to climb up on the roof of Donut Hearts without being seen and do it."

A sudden thought occurred to me. "What if they hadn't gone up there originally with the intention of committing murder?"

"Why else would anyone climb up there, then?"

"What if they saw the ladder and knew that Cassandra was meeting someone there? Could they have been there just to spy on her, with no intention of killing her initially?"

"I don't know," Phillip said, scratching his chin in thought.

"It's pretty outlandish, isn't it?" I asked him.

"Not necessarily. At this point, I don't think any theory is too crazy to consider," Phillip admitted. "Let's jump into my truck and find Mary before someone else tells her the news."

CHAPTER 11

"**M**ARY, WE NEED TO TALK," I said as she came to the door of the house she'd been cleaning. The housekeeper had been fairly easy to find, given her bright-yellow van with the Eiffel Tower painted on its side, adorned with the words For the Very Best, Choose Paris. It was catchy; I had to give her that.

"What is it you want?" she asked, looking at us both sternly. "I'm working."

"We just thought you might like to know that the pin Cassandra accused you of stealing has been found," I said, watching her eyes. Did they dilate a fraction when she heard the news, or was it just my imagination?

"I'm not surprised," Mary said after composing herself for a moment. "I've said all along that I didn't take it."

"True. Your reputation means a great deal to you, doesn't it?" Phillip asked her.

"It is everything," Mary admitted.

"Enough to take drastic measures to protect it?" I asked, pushing in closer to her.

"I have no idea what you're talking about. I'm just sorry Cassandra Lane isn't alive so I can make her apologize to me publicly."

Catching us both off guard, Phillip asked her gently, "You're not afraid of heights, are you, Mary?"

"What? Of course not. I clean light fixtures twenty feet in the air every week. Why do you ask?"

"Well, whoever cut the wires on that donut had to climb up a ladder in back of Donut Hearts," he said. "It's good to know that you could have done it."

"I didn't kill anyone," she said in a high, shrill voice. Without another word, she went back into the house, slamming the door behind her.

"Wow, that woman's got a bit of a temper," I said to Phillip as we made our way back to his truck.

"Not only that, but she admitted that she was no stranger to heights."

"That was clever asking her that," I said.

"I have my moments," Phillip replied. "I'm in the mood to grill a few of our other suspects. How about you?"

"I'm all for it," I said. "First up, we need to find Bernie Nance and Heather Lindquist."

"The lady might be a problem, but I can get us a little help finding Bernie."

"How is that?" I asked.

"The chief in Maple Hollow owes me a favor, and since that's where Bernie has been holing up, I think it's time to collect."

An hour later, we were parked across the street from a convenience store on the outskirts of Maple Hollow. "Are you sure he's in there?" I asked Phillip.

"That's his beat-up old Chevy, according to my source," he said. "He's working there part time, so he had to check in with the police department, since he's still on parole."

"So, why aren't we going in?" I asked.

There was only one other car in the store parking lot, and a moment later, a pretty young long-legged brunette left with a troubled expression on her face. A creepy little man had his face pressed against the window, watching her as she climbed into her car. He was taking her in as though she was some kind of piece of prime beef, not a person with her own hopes and dreams.

"I haven't even met this guy yet and he gives me the creeps," I said as Phillip started the truck. "Where are we going?"

"We're going to go have a little chat with Bernie."

"Do we have to?" I asked, not relishing the thought of even being in this man's presence.

"It's not like I'm sending you in alone, but if you'd rather sit this one out, that's okay with me. I can handle him."

What was I suddenly being so squeamish about? It wasn't as though I was some kind of naïve teenager. For goodness sake, I was a twice-married woman! "I'm fine. Let's go have a chat with Bernie."

"If you're sure," he said as he parked and got out.

I followed close behind, happy that I had my stepfather with me, even if it was a bit irrational.

"I don't want trouble with no cops," Bernie said the second Phillip walked into the convenience store. What was it that had given him away as a former officer of the law without him even having to open his mouth?

"Then tell the truth and you'll be fine," Phillip said, his voice shifting into a tone that I recognized in Jake's on occasion. He called it his "cop voice," and I wasn't entirely sure that he always knew when he was using it.

"I'm not saying a word without my attorney," Bernie said. He was an undersized little man in need of a haircut and most likely a good scrubbing, not that I was going to volunteer to give him either one.

Phillip just stood there, and I took my cue from him, remaining silent.

After a full minute ticked off the clock, Bernie broke first. "I didn't do it."

"Do what?" Phillip asked him coolly.

"Anything that would bring you by here," the ex-con said sullenly.

"Tell us about Cassandra Lane," I said, which may have been a mistake. Up until that point, he'd only given me a cursory glance, but that brought his full focus on me. I knew full well that I was anything but a glamour model, but the way he sized me up made me shiver a little deep down. I'd met men like him before once or twice, and dealing with them had always left me cold and afraid.

"She's the reason for my problems," he finally said, still staring intently at me. "Why do you care? Is she complaining about me again? I never got within five hundred feet of her, no matter what she says. I know better than to break a restraining order. If she's got a problem with me, she can come and tell me to my face."

"That would be a little hard to do, given the court order and all," Phillip said. "Where were you last night between seven and nine p.m.?"

"I was home," he said. "It was my normal shift here, but I wasn't feeling so good, so I called in sick."

"Can anyone vouch for you?" I asked.

Again he gave me the look that made me want to go straight home and take a long, hot shower. "No. I was all by my lonesome. You want to come by tonight when I get off and change that?"

I was so startled by his lewd invitation that I didn't even know how to respond. Fortunately, I didn't have to. Phillip slammed his palm down on the counter and got perilously close to Bernie's face. "Don't even look at her again. I will put you in the ground if you do. Do you understand me?" My stepfather was genuinely angry, something that touched my heart.

"I didn't mean nothing by it," Bernie said sullenly as he stared down at his hands.

"Now we know that you had motive, means, and opportunity," Phillip said.

"I don't even know what it was I was supposed to have done," Bernie whined.

"You killed Cassandra Lane," I said, watching him carefully for some kind of reaction, hoping to catch any subtle and nuanced change in his demeanor.

His sudden burst of laughter and obvious glee caught me completely by surprise.

"She's dead? Somebody killed her?" he asked, barely able to contain his glee. "Well, they sure saved me the trouble, and the jail time!" He tore off his uniform shirt, revealing a dirty once-white T-shirt underneath, and slammed it on the counter.

"What do you think you're doing?" Phillip asked him, clearly as startled as I had been by the man's reaction.

"There's no reason for me to stay now," Bernie said, "so unless you're planning on arresting me, I'm taking off."

"You're going to just leave the place open like this?" I asked.

"They can keep my last paycheck," he said as he walked out the door, whistling.

"Do we follow him?" I asked Phillip.

"I don't think so. Did that reaction strike you as well-thought-out and expertly acted, Suzanne?"

"I can't imagine that man doing anything more complicated than tying his shoes," I admitted.

"I agree. He was genuinely surprised that Cassandra was dead. I don't think he's our man."

After giving it some thought, I nodded. "I agree. He's a dead end. To be honest with you, I'm glad he's not on our list anymore. That guy gave me the creeps in a big way. By the way, thanks for defending me."

"It was nothing," Phillip said, frowning at the situation. "We need to call the store owner and get someone over here right away. We can't just let this place get looted because Bernie decided to leave town suddenly."

I walked behind the register and found a note mounted to a piece of cardboard. It said, "If you can't figure something out, call me. Do not try to fix it yourself!" Evidently the shop owner had had problems with employees before. I knew there were different types of convenience stores. One I went to on occasion in April Springs was always clean and organized, its staff cheerful and helpful. This was the other type of place. I couldn't imagine the last time the floor had been mopped, and it was a wonder anyone could see out of the windows at all for all the grime built up on them. I called the number, and after a dozen rings, a woman answered in a frazzled voice, "This is Melinda."

"Melinda, I'm Suzanne Hart. I'm at your convenience store in Maple Hollow."

"I don't remember hiring anyone named Suzanne," she said, the weariness thick in her voice.

"You didn't. I was here with a friend and your clerk took his shirt off and walked out."

The poor woman didn't even seem surprised to hear my news. "Is Bernie really gone, then?"

"Yes, and unfortunately, I doubt that he'll ever be back," I said. "What should we do?"

"Celebrate," Melinda said, clearly happy to hear the news. "I'm ten minutes away. Could you possibly stay until I get there?"

"Of course," I said even without consulting Phillip. After all, we small business owners needed to stick together, even if I didn't approve of the state of her convenience store.

While we stood there waiting, a woman came in and asked

for a pack of gum. I sold it to her and made change while Phillip looked on, amused.

After she was gone, he said with a smile, "I didn't realize you were on the clock."

"Do you mind? It won't be long, and I hate for her to lose any business. It doesn't appear that she can afford to."

"I don't mind a bit," he said as he leaned against the window.

I waited on a few more customers, sold a little gas, and soon enough, a woman in her late fifties came in, looking around for her AWOL clerk, just in case he'd decided to come back. She looked a little surprised to find me behind the counter. "Is it true? Is he really gone?"

"He is," I said as I offered my hand. "I'm Suzanne Hart, and that's Phillip Martin."

"It's a pleasure to meet you both. Thanks so much for staying." She walked around the counter, took my place and hit NO SALE, then gave the till a quick check.

"If anything's missing, Bernie probably took it on his way out," I said. "You can check the security footage if you don't believe me," I said as I pointed to a camera overhead with its flashing red light.

"That's just a dummy to keep people honest," she admitted. "I didn't mean to make it look as though I didn't trust you. I'm just so relieved that he's gone."

"Ma'am, if you don't mind me asking, if you didn't like Bernie, why did you hire him in the first place?" Phillip asked.

"I didn't. My husband did, an hour before I caught him cheating with one of our other clerks, Haley Sue. I threw them both out, but when I tried to fire Bernie, he said he wasn't going anywhere. I threatened to call the police, but he told me I'd regret it if I did. I'm not afraid to tell you that man scared the daylights out of me!"

Phillip jotted something down on a slip of paper. "This is my number. If you get into another jam, call me."

"Are you a police officer?"

"I used to be, and I'd be happy to help you," Phillip said.

I had never been prouder of the man my mother had married than I was at that moment.

Melinda nodded her thanks as she looked around the store. "I've been afraid to come here and clean up, but now that he's gone, I can give this place a proper scrubbing."

"We'd be happy to stick around and help," I said. Phillip shook his head in wonder at my invitation, but I could see a smile begin to peek through as well.

"No need. I'll call my sisters, and we'll have this place spotless in no time." Turning back to the open register, she reached for a few twenties. "I would greatly appreciate it if you'd take a reward for your kindness."

I didn't even have to think about that. "There's no need. We can't accept money for doing what we hope someone would do for us."

Melinda frowned, and then she tore off a few scratch-off lottery tickets. "Will you at least take two of these? I have to give you something."

I was about to refuse when Phillip stepped forward. "We appreciate that, ma'am," he said as he took them, and then handed them both to me. One shake of his head told me not to protest any further.

"Thank you," I said.

"I should be the one thanking you," she said with a grin.

Out in the parking lot, I turned to Phillip. "That was sweet of you to give her your number, but why did you take the lottery tickets?"

"Couldn't you see the look in her eyes? She had to give us something. It wasn't for us, Suzanne, it was for her."

I thought about it, and then I tore the two tickets on their perforated line. "You take one, and I'll take the other," I said. "After all, you were there, too."

Phillip looked at the extended ticket, and then he laughed as he shoved it into his shirt pocket, bending one corner as he did so. "I don't suppose I have any way to refuse, now do I?"

"No, sir," I said. "So, Bernie is off our list, and so is Shelly Hastings. That just leaves us with Marybeth Jenkins, Richard Beacon, Heather Lindquist, and Mary Paris. At least we're narrowing the field down a bit."

"I suppose so," he said. "Since we've already spoken to Mary, that leaves Marybeth, Heather, and Richard."

"Don't forget, I've spoken with Marybeth," I said. "We can always go back to her, but I think for now we should concentrate on Richard and Heather."

"That sounds like a plan. Unfortunately, I don't know where either one of them is at the moment, besides the fact that the contractor is working somewhere in Union Square. It's a big place, and we can't just drive around looking for his work truck. Do you have any suggestions as to how we might find them?"

"I'll think about it on the ride back to April Springs," I said.

"Are we heading back now?" he asked me.

"Clearly we need to go to Union Square. We can check out the Claremont Inn and then see if we can track Richard Beacon down."

"What about Heather Lindquist?" he asked.

"Do we have any reason to believe she's here in Maple Hollow?" I asked him.

"No. I asked the chief here, but he'd never heard of her. He did a quick search on her name, and he couldn't find any indication that she'd ever been in town."

"So there's not much use for us to look for her here," I said.

"Suzanne, just because someone's path hasn't crossed the police's doesn't mean that they aren't around."

"No, but if the chief here doesn't know about her, what are the odds *we* can find her? Let's focus right now on what we can do, not what we can't."

"That sounds logical enough to me," the chief said. "We have to go back through April Springs to get to Union Square, so when we do, I want to shift over to your Jeep."

"What's wrong? Are you getting tired of chauffeuring me around?" I asked him with a smile.

"No, but I want to make some phone calls while we're on the road. I have more connections I can use to help us find our suspects."

"That works for me," I said as he headed back home.

I hoped Phillip could work his magic again. I hadn't realized, though I should have, that my stepfather still had so many active sources in the area. Why shouldn't he, though? After all, he'd been the chief of police in April Springs for quite a while.

Maybe, just maybe, one of his sources would pay off and we'd be able to find our remaining suspects.

CHAPTER 12

A S WE WERE DRIVING BACK to April Springs, my phone rang. I was about to hit the IGNORE button when I saw that it was my husband!

"Jake! How are you?"

"I'm good. I just have a second, but I wanted to check in."

"How's the job going?" I asked him.

"It's complicated," he answered a bit mysteriously for my taste. "Are you doing okay?"

"I'm fine," I said. I didn't want to trouble him with Cassandra's murder while he was working, and besides, it wasn't as though I was sleuthing alone. I had a former chief of police working the case with me, so how much safer could I be?

"Good to hear that. Listen, I'm sorry this is so rushed, but I've got to go. Stay safe."

"You, too," I said as he killed the connection.

"You didn't tell him about Cassandra," Phillip said after a moment.

"You heard how brief our conversation was. There just wasn't time."

"There was time enough to tell him that," Phillip said after another few moments of silence.

I took a deep breath and then let it out slowly. "I didn't see any reason to worry him. Jake's got enough to deal with without being concerned about me. It's okay."

"Okay, if that works for you, then it's none of my business," Phillip said, clearly just trying to mollify me.

"I'm curious about something now. Did you tell Momma what we were up to?" I asked after stewing for a minute or two.

"As a matter of fact, I called her while we were dropping your Jeep off at Donut Hearts," he said.

Blast it all, he'd have to be considerate of his own spouse, wouldn't he? "What did she say?"

"She's glad we're working together," he answered. "She worries about you, Suzanne."

"I know, but it's kind of crazy. I'm a grown woman, after all."

He chewed on that for a moment before answering. "True, but in her eyes, you'll always be her little girl."

"Well, I'm glad you could allay her fears."

"Honestly, I'm not sure that I did," he said. "Now she's worried about *both* of us."

I looked over at him, and I couldn't help myself. I started to chuckle. "I'm sorry. I know it's not funny."

"Well, maybe a little," Phillip said with the hint of a smile. "We don't need to share the fact that we find it amusing with your mother though, do we?"

"I'll make you a deal. I won't say anything if you won't," I said.

By the time we got back to April Springs, my stomach started growling. "Are you hungry at all?" I asked Phillip.

"I'm starving," he said with a grin. "I didn't think you'd ever ask. That donut didn't hold me."

"Hey, you could have said something yourself."

"It's your investigation. I'm the support person here, but now that you've brought it up, can we take a little time to get something to eat?"

"How does the Boxcar sound to you?" I asked.

"Like a home run," he said.

Two minutes later, we were parked beside my Jeep in front of Donut Hearts, and after a short stroll across the street, we were at the diner.

When we walked in together, Trish's eyebrows shot up, but only for a moment. "Fancy seeing you two together," she said. "What brings you to my humble establishment together?"

"Can't I have a late lunch with my mother's husband without attracting attention?" I asked her with a smile.

"Suzanne, what fun would that be if I couldn't even tease you? Sit wherever you want, you've both caught me in a bit of a lull."

"You don't have to tell me about lulls," I said with a sigh.

Trish frowned and dropped her chin down, making her ever-present ponytail bounce a little. "I'm sorry I said that; it was a poor choice of words. I wish I had some sage advice to give you, but all I can say is to keep your chin up, hang in there, and keep swinging."

"Wow, that's a fair number of clichés all strung together in a long piece of advice."

"Hey, they're clichés for a reason," she said. "Now what can I get you? Since you're loitering here at the front, I might as well take your order." She winked at me, showing that she was just teasing, and I just laughed.

"I'd love a burger all the way and fries, and I wouldn't say no to some sweet tea, either," I said.

"Make that two," Phillip said.

Trish nodded as she jotted our order down, and then she had to step away to cash out a bill.

After we took a table near one of the windows, Phillip said, "You haven't mentioned to your mother and me that you were having trouble at Donut Hearts."

"It's nothing for anyone to worry about. I'm working on

turning things around," I said, not really wanting to discuss my financial woes with my stepfather.

"You know, I've got a little money of my own put away. You're welcome to whatever you need," he said softly so that no one around us would hear his suggestion.

I patted his hand and gave him my brightest smile. "I appreciate the offer, Phillip, but I'm fine. Really."

"Your mother wouldn't have to know," he persisted.

"Like I said, I've got a plan."

"Okay, I get it," he said. Almost as an afterthought, he started to pull out his wallet.

"Hey, I just said that I don't want any money," I said a little stronger than I probably should have.

"That's good, because I'm not giving you any. Take this," he said as he shoved the lottery ticket toward me. "I put it away for safe keeping, but you can use it more than I can. I hope you have lucky numbers! Look at that. I just doubled your odds of winning."

I grinned and took the offered ticket. "Yes, now it's only a million-to-one chance of me winning anything versus two million to one like before. I feel richer already," I replied as I tucked the ticket into my wallet beside the other one. "Yours has a crease in one corner."

"Don't worry, they'll still cash it if you win," he said with a smile.

"Thanks. I appreciate the gesture." It was time to change the subject. "Have you been working on any good cold cases lately?" My stepfather was getting rather good at acting as his own cold-case team, and Jake and I loved hearing about his latest investigations.

"As a matter of fact, there's something that caught my eye when I was studying a batch of old newspapers the other day. Did you know that a shipment of gold was stolen not ten miles from here in the late 1800s? They never did find out what happened to it or even who took it."

"Are you actually treasure hunting now?" I asked as Trish brought us a pair of sweet teas without even stopping to eavesdrop on our conversation. She must have had something going on up front, or else I knew she'd have taken a seat at our table to hear more about it.

"Two men were killed in the course of the robbery, so that's what first piqued my interest. If I find a trace of the money, I believe I'll find the killer."

"What makes you think it's even still around here?"

"That's the interesting part," he explained. "Five years after the theft and the murders, two coins showed up in town, totally unexpected."

"Who tried to spend them? Wouldn't that lead the authorities to finding the killer?" I couldn't help myself. Phillip had sucked me into the case without my consent. That was what curiosity got for me.

"That's the thing. They weren't actually spent. They were donated to the orphanage that used to be on the outskirts of town. It's significant because one of the guards they killed was a widower, and his kids ended up in that very same orphanage. My guess is that the thief had a bout of conscience and tried to make a little restitution to some of those he hurt."

"Is there anything I can do to help you with the case?" I asked. "It sounds intriguing."

"Right now I'm still digging around in the old newspapers for any more leads, but if I think of something you can do, I'll let you know." He paused a moment for a sip of sweet tea before adding, "I appreciate your interest in the case. Your mother thinks I'm a little too obsessed about crimes that happened so long ago in the past, especially since it's probably much too late to bring anyone to justice."

"Just knowing what really happened is enough though, isn't it? You might not be able to bring a killer in, but you can give the victims' families some peace of mind about what really happened all those years ago. It's a worthy way to spend your retirement if you ask me."

Phillip and I had just finished eating when I looked up to see a woman staring at me from across the room. She didn't look familiar, but contrary to popular belief, I didn't know every soul who passed through April Springs. As a matter of fact, I didn't even know all of our townsfolk. If they didn't love donuts, there was a chance our paths might not ever even cross.

She caught me looking back at her, but instead of being embarrassed, she frowned as she walked over to our table. A petite pale blonde in her late twenties, she had a bit of an elfin quality to her.

"Excuse me. Am I interrupting something?" she asked me, glancing over at Phillip for a moment as well.

"No, we were just finishing our meal. Was there something I could help you with?"

"I'm hoping so," she said. "You're the donut lady, aren't you?"

I'd certainly been called a lot worse. "I'm Suzanne Hart Bishop," I said, offering my hand to her, "and this is Phillip Martin, my stepfather." I usually didn't introduce myself that way since most folks knew me as just Hart, but I liked the sound of my full married name, so I used it occasionally. As for Phillip, I was beginning to realize that it was high time I accepted the fact that not only was he in my mother's life, he was a part of mine as well.

"You solve crimes around here too, is that right?" she asked.

"I've been known to dig into them from time to time," I admitted. "I'm sorry, but I didn't catch your name."

"Perhaps that's because I didn't give it," she said with a partial smile. "I'm Heather Lindquist. May I sit down?"

"By all means," I said. Sometimes life worked that way. We'd had this woman on our list to track down, and here she was, dropping herself right into our laps without a hint of effort on our part.

"Would you like something to eat?" Phillip asked. "I can tell Trish if you'd like."

"Nothing for me, thanks. I don't think I could eat a bite." She turned back to me and said, "I was hoping you could help me."

"In what way?" I asked.

"The local police chief wants to talk to me, and I'm a little nervous about the entire situation."

"Well, correct me if I'm wrong, but you *did* threaten Cassandra on more than one occasion, didn't you?" Phillip asked her.

"What can I say? I was angry with her," Heather said, her soft features hardening for a moment. "I know now that she was just doing her job, but I held her responsible for my brother's killer literally getting away with murder."

"So, you admit that you had a motive," Phillip said. Wow, it hadn't taken long for his "cop voice" to kick in.

"I would *never* have done such a thing," she said indignantly. "Taking a life is wrong, no matter who is doing it. Besides, I *couldn't* have done it, not if what I've heard about the way Ms. Lane died is at all true."

"What did you hear?" I asked her.

"Apparently someone pushed a giant donut on top of her from the roof of your shop," she said, "as incredible as that may sound."

"Trust me, I saw her body crushed on the sidewalk in front of Donut Hearts. There's not much chance of me ever forgetting it."

"I'm sorry. I didn't mean to be insensitive."

She was certainly one of the politest suspects I'd ever had, a sharp contrast to Bernie Nance. That didn't make her innocent of the accused crime, though. "You see, that clears me completely. I could *never* have gone up on that roof. I'm terrified of heights. As a matter of fact, I won't even go up on a stepstool. There is no way I could ever climb a ladder and walk across your roof."

"I'm afraid we don't have anyone's word for that but yours now, do we?" I asked her.

"Are you saying that you don't *believe* me?" She looked absolutely incredulous that anyone would ever question her word.

"I'm just saying that without more substantial proof than that, the police chief has every right to interview you. My advice is to go talk to the man and tell him your story. If all else fails, the truth is at the very least easier to remember."

She stood up, looking hurt. "I come to you for help, and you call me a liar?"

"Take it easy," Phillip said as we both stood as well. "Nobody's accusing you of anything."

"I don't know why I bothered. You're no help at all!" Heather hurried out of the diner as Trish was approaching with our bill, and I worried for her safety for a moment. Heather might be tiny, but she appeared to have the heart of a lion when she felt threatened, something to remember when it came time to evaluate our suspects.

"Was it something I said?" Trish asked as she handed Phillip the bill and watched as the door swung shut.

"No, I believe it was something *I* said," I answered. I gestured to the bill. "I'll pay half that, if you don't mind."

"Actually, you're our hundredth customer today," Trish said

with a grin. "That entitles you to a buy one/get one free deal." She smiled at Phillip. "Sorry, but you're the one paying for your own meal."

"I'm happy to do it," he said as he reached for his wallet.

"Trish, I don't take anyone's charity," I said with a hint of steel in my voice.

"I'll take it if she doesn't want it," Jackson, a teller from my bank, said from a nearby table.

"Sorry, but you don't qualify," Trish said sweetly.

"Patricia Louise Granger," I said sternly, staring into her eyes with the hardest gaze I had.

"Suzanne Hart Bishop," she replied, trying to be just as stark but failing miserably as she broke into a smile. "Just let me have this one, okay?" she asked softly.

"Fine, but you're getting some donuts on the house tomorrow, and I don't want to hear a word of protest from you. Is that understood?"

"Understood, and greatly appreciated," she said.

After Trish went back up front to grab another order, I looked at Phillip. "I'm getting the tip, and I don't want to hear a word out of you."

"I wasn't about to protest," he said with a grin. "Come on. Let's get out of here. That's just about all of the craziness I can take at the moment. Why don't we head over to Union Square and see what we can uncover about Cassandra Lane's killer?"

"That sounds like a plan to me," I said, and after he paid our bill and I left a very generous tip, we were off in my Jeep in pursuit of a cold-blooded killer who had dared to use something attached to my donut shop as a murder weapon.

It wasn't just Cassandra's lost life, or George's potential lost freedom.

It was personal.

CHAPTER 13

As I drove us to Union Square in my Jeep, Phillip pulled out his cell phone. "Who exactly are you calling, anyway? I can't imagine the kind of connections you must have after being the police chief for so long."

"As a matter of fact, my first call is to someone you know pretty well yourself," he said.

"Well, don't keep me in suspense," I said. "Tell me."

"Just listen," Phillip said as he finished dialing the number. "George, do you have a second?"

Was he really calling the mayor? If so, why hadn't he put the call on speakerphone so I could take part in it as well? It was too late to ask now, so I just drove on and tried my best to eavesdrop.

From Phillip's side of the conversation, I heard him say, "Sure. Listen, I'm thinking about taking Dot out of town for a little getaway. Do you know anything about the Claremont Inn?" There was a pause, and he frowned for a moment before he spoke again. "So, you've never been there yourself. Yes, I know I can do better. It was just a thought. Anyway, thanks." It was clear that he wanted to get off the phone, but George wouldn't let him. "We're making progress, but that's all that I can say right now. Okay," he said as he glanced over at me. "Yes, we'll be in touch. Tonight. Bye."

After Phillip hung up the phone, I said, "You know, putting that on speaker might have been nice."

127

"If I had, you would have wanted to be a part of the conversation. Am I right?" Phillip asked.

"I might have had something to add," I admitted.

"That's what I figured. I didn't want it to be a thing, Suzanne. This way it was quick and painless, straight to the point."

"Are you saying that I go off on tangents when I'm on the phone?" I asked him. "Be very careful as to how you answer that."

"This needed to be more like a man-to-man conversation," Phillip said. "I'm sorry. I should have at least told you what I was doing."

I suddenly realized that I was being a little petulant about the whole thing with no real cause to feel slighted. "No worries. I'm the one who should be apologizing. That was a clever way of finding out if he'd been at the Claremont with Cassandra."

"It proved your point about one keepsake per relationship, at any rate," Phillip said. "I still can't help wondering who it was she met there."

"Maybe if we dig around a little, we can find out," I said.

"I can't afford too many cash bribes, and since you're out of donuts, we can't get those to give the staff a reason to speak with us," Phillip said.

"Don't you worry about that. One of their front desk clerks is a good customer of mine," I said. Billy Summers came into the donut shop once a week, making the trip all the way from Union Square just for my goodies. I was flattered, but then again, I made the drive to Napoli's to get Angelica's delightful cuisine, so I could relate. "I just hope he's on duty."

"Should I call ahead to check?" Phillip asked me.

"No, we need to go there anyway. It will just make things a great deal easier if Billy's on duty. Do you have any more calls to make before we get there?"

"A few," he said. "Do you mind if I don't put them on

speaker, either? If it helps, you don't know any of them, at least I don't think you do. Besides, your Jeep can get a little noisy driving down the road."

"I like to think that's part of its charm," I said.

"Okay then, there are times when your Jeep can be *very* charming." He said it with a smile, so I decided to take it with one as well. It was well-known among my family and friends that I was very defensive about my mode of transportation. I knew that a Jeep wasn't the most practical mode of transportation I could drive, but I loved how fun it was, and after all, did I really need any more reason than that?

As I drove, I tried to listen in on Phillip's other conversations, but it was difficult to hear what was being said on the other end of the line. Still, I managed to piece a few clues together from his questions and comments.

Nearing the entrance to the Claremont Inn, Phillip finally put his cell phone away. "I can't believe we ever managed without these things," he said.

"They can be a blessing *and* a curse, as far as I'm concerned," I said. "I love to be able to chat with Jake whenever I need to, but sometimes I feel as though the thing owns me and not the other way around. The other day I left the cottage without it, and so help me, I turned right around to go back and get it. I wouldn't last a shift at work without having it with me. Honestly, I felt kind of pathetic being so dependent on it."

"Sometimes I leave mine plugged into the charger for days without ever even using it," Phillip said smugly.

"But Momma always has hers on her, doesn't she?" I asked.

He frowned for a moment. "Yes, I hadn't really thought of it that way."

As I parked in the visitors' lot, I looked around at the other vehicles there. I saw a wide range of automobiles and trucks, from the latest BMW to an old Ford pickup I was amazed had even made it out of the driveway.

Phillip and I walked in side by side, and the clerk behind the desk—not Billy, sadly—asked, "Welcome to the Claremont. How many nights will you be staying with us?"

"We're not here looking for a room," I said hurriedly. "We're not together that way. He's my stepfather." I was talking way too much, and I noticed that Phillip was frowning at me. "Is Billy working today?"

"He'll be in soon," the young woman said, dismissing us with barely another glance.

"We'll just wait over there, then," I said, pointing to some orange chairs that were supposed to be comfortable by design.

They were not.

After we sat, I glanced over at Phillip, who was still clearly unhappy about something. "Don't worry. We have time to wait on Billy."

"Sure," he grunted.

"Is something wrong?"

"Suzanne, it's not completely out of the question that a man my age could be with a woman of yours. You made it sound as though it was the most preposterous thing in the world that we might be together."

I had to choke back a laugh at the mere thought of it. I'd clearly hurt the poor man's feelings. "Phillip, she just caught me off guard. You're married to my mother, for goodness sake."

"We both know that, but she didn't," Phillip said, a bit of the chill coming out of his voice, though it was still a little frosty.

"I'm sorry. I didn't think," I said. Not only was that true, but I hadn't meant to dismiss him in any way. "Do you forgive me?"

I gave him my biggest doe-eyed look I could, and after holding his frown for a moment, he finally broke out into a smile. "Stop it."

"I really am truly very sorry. Any girl would be lucky to be with a man as handsome and as virile as you clearly are," I said, emphasizing the words much more than was called for by the situation.

"Okay, I get it," he said, now chuckling as well. "We're both pretty, pretty girls, anybody would be lucky to be with either one of us. Hey, is that your friend by any chance?" he asked as Billy walked in, dressed in the company blazer that marked their front-desk employees. Billy was an example of overindulgence, not just in my donuts, but in most things culinary, and he had the outline to prove it.

"Suzanne? What are you doing here?" he asked as he paused at my chair. "It's not donut day, and as far as I know, you don't deliver."

"Billy, do you have a second?" I asked.

"Sure, but give me a minute," he said as he walked to the desk, moved behind it, and had a brief conversation with the woman he was replacing, but only after he tapped a few keys on the computer first, no doubt punching in for the day. I was glad I didn't have to worry about time clocks or punch-ins, but then I realized that I worked many more hours a week than someone on a company payroll would. I'd once heard it said that a self-employed person would rather work eighty hours a week for themselves than forty for someone else, and without exception, I'd found it to be true.

After he relieved his coworker and he checked on a few things, Billy motioned us over to the desk. "I have a few minutes. What's up?" he asked as he glanced at Phillip.

"This is Phillip Martin. He's a friend of mine," I said.

"Actually, I'm her stepfather," he said with a smile as he offered his hand.

Billy took it briefly. "What can I do for you?"

"I need some information," I said as I pulled out my cell

phone and brought up the photo I'd taken of the receipt I'd found at Cassandra's place. "Can you tell me anything about this?"

He glanced at my screen, and then he shook his head. After looking back over his shoulder, he turned back to me and said in a loud voice, "Sorry, but our guests' stays here are strictly confidential."

"Okay. I get it. I just thought I would ask," I said. "Thanks, anyway."

Billy nodded, and then he jotted something down on a sheet of paper, clearly dismissing us. I must have overstepped my bounds with him, which could happen at times when I was investigating a murder. I'd have to cover his next donut order on the house to make up for it.

Phillip and I were nearly at the door when Billy called out, "Ma'am, I believe you dropped something."

I looked at him, puzzled. "Excuse me?"

He waved the piece of paper he'd written on earlier in his hand. "I'm sure this is yours," he said, his eyes urging me to play along.

Then I heard someone behind him, someone I hadn't seen at that point. "Is there a problem, William?" a severe-looking woman asked. She was dressed in a much nicer suit than the blazer Billy was wearing, and she was clearly in charge.

"Just trying to do a good deed, ma'am," Billy said as he waved me back.

"Very well, but I'm going to need those reports very soon." This was not a request but clearly an order.

I hurried back and took the paper from his hands. "Sorry about that. I'm so clumsy sometimes."

"It's absolutely not a problem," he said, winking at me out of the woman's line of sight. "Please consider us here at the Claremont Inn during your next trip to Union Square."

"I will certainly do that. Thank you for your sterling customer service," I added, hoping to get him some brownie points with his boss.

Billy rolled his eyes when he heard my comment, and Phillip and I left the lobby of the inn.

"What's on the paper?" Phillip asked me once we were outside.

"Come back and see me at six," I read from the note. "Maybe I can help." It was clear that Billy wasn't at liberty to talk, but I had hopes that he might give us something about Cassandra's mystery rendezvous. "It looks as though we're hanging around Union Square a little longer than we expected to," I said as I folded the note and put it in my pocket. "Did you have any luck tracking Richard Beacon down? We know that he's working in Union Square, but that covers a lot of ground. A specific address might be helpful."

"While you were chatting with Billy, I got a text from one of my contacts. Apparently Richard is working on the Haversom House on Longview Road."

"Wow, you really do have some network of connections, don't you?" I asked.

"Doing what I did for so long, it would be hard not to. Do you know where Longview Road is? I can call it up on my phone."

"That would be nice," I said. "I suppose that's another item for the plus column for cell phones. It's much tougher to get lost than it was before they came along."

"But still not impossible," Phillip said as we listened to the directions together. A soothing voice told us that we were three point seven miles away, so fairly soon we'd be speaking with another suspect in Cassandra Lane's murder.

The man standing in front of the contractor's trailer glared at us as I pulled my Jeep in right behind it. It was fairly clear that he wasn't happy about our presence, and he didn't even know yet that we were there to grill him about murder. "Phillip, play along with me," I said as I started to get out of the Jeep.

My stepfather looked at me with a confused expression on his face, and I hoped that he could hold up his end of my pending ruse. If it had been Grace, there would have been no problem with us both playacting to get information. In fact, she preferred it when we did that, but my stepfather was another matter altogether. Oh, well. I'd made my decision about the best way to approach the man, and there was no going back now.

"Are you Richard Beacon?" I asked him as innocently as I could manage.

He pointed to the side of his trailer, where his name was emblazoned in bright-red letters, along with an outline of a lighthouse. Actually, that was pretty clever. "That's me. What can I do for you?" He was covered in sawdust, and three discarded boards lay on the ground. Had he miscut them, or were they cast-offs, remnants of his current work? Based on his irritability with us, my bet was on the former.

"We understand you do remodeling," I said. I must have sounded like an idiot, but I had to get the conversation going, and Phillip was no help. He just stood there with a dopey grin on his face.

"What do you need?" he asked again.

"I'd love to get a quote. I spoke with a friend of mine when you started a project for her, and she highly recommended you," I said.

"What's your friend's name?" The contractor looked pleased as he asked the question.

"Cassandra Lane," Phillip blurted out.

I might have been a little more subtle about it, but my

stepfather's bluntness might be just the ticket to an honest reaction to the dead attorney's name. Richard Beacon's smile suddenly vanished. "She didn't recommend me to anyone, and even if she did, I wouldn't take the job. I don't care what she says. I did the work she requested, she changed her mind at the last second, and then she refused to pay me. I'm getting that money out of her one way or the other."

"It might be difficult at this point," I said. "Someone murdered her last night."

"Really," he said, the tone and pitch of his voice not changing in the slightest. "That doesn't really concern me. If she wouldn't pay me while she was alive, I can guarantee you that her estate will."

"Exactly how much money are we talking about here?" Phillip asked. That question never would have occurred to me, and I was glad that he was along.

"Seven hundred sixty-eight dollars and thirty-four cents," he said.

"Really? I thought it would be more than that," I said. Would someone actually commit murder over that amount of money?

"I tiled her laundry room. She wasn't happy about the pattern toward the back, even though she'd agreed to it before I even got started. She thought it looked a little off. Guess what? She paid for a random pattern! To beat it all, the only spot she had a problem with was going to be under the dryer, anyway! No one was ever going to see it! I'm going to get paid for that job one way or another."

He certainly sounded angry enough about the conflict. The man clearly had a temper. But still, I couldn't imagine taking someone's life over less than a thousand dollars, and this murder had been cold and calculating. After all, someone had climbed up onto the roof of my shop and cut those supporting cables, and then they'd pushed the fiberglass donut when Cassandra was in precisely the right spot. If she'd been stabbed or even run over by a car, this man would be a legitimate suspect, but something about him just didn't ring true as a premeditated killer.

Phillip asked him, "Have you been sued many times before?"

"All in all, four times," he said. "They all ended up paying, one way or the other," he added ominously.

"What do you mean?" I asked.

"Three were settled before the cases went before the judge, and I won the fourth one."

"But you lost to Cassandra Lane," I reminded him. "That would make it five times you've been sued."

"She knew the judge! There was no way I was getting a fair shake out of that," he said. "You know what? It's not worth it. By the time I go through the hassle of collecting from her estate, I'll probably lose more money than I stand to gain. As for the two of you, I'm not interested in your business. Any friend of that woman is no friend of mine."

He turned back to his saw and flipped it on, effectively ending our conversation, so at that point, we really had no choice but to leave.

Back in the Jeep, I started the engine, turned around, and then I headed back into Union Square proper. "Phillip, I don't think he did it."

"I don't, either," my stepfather said. "If she'd been shot, I'd be on board, but the man isn't clever enough to premeditate a grocery shopping list."

"I thought about stabbing or vehicular homicide, but your point is the same as mine. Who is there still on our list who *might* be that cunning?" I asked him.

"Heather could have done it," he said. "There's more to that woman bubbling under the surface than meets the eye."

"I hate to say it, but Marybeth might do something like it, too. If she thought she was protecting George, she might have come up with a way to kill Cassandra and not be seen doing it."

"How about Mary Paris?" Phillip asked.

"She might have done it, too," I conceded. "After all, she's certainly not afraid of heights. She admitted that much to us herself," I said.

"Do you honestly believe that *Heather* is afraid of heights?" Phillip asked me as I passed by Napoli's. If we hadn't just eaten at the Boxcar a few hours earlier, I might have been tempted, but I knew that if I put myself in Angelica's care, I'd be so stuffed that I'd never get to sleep that night. "We only have her word on that, and if you ask me, it seemed awfully convenient as an excuse."

"Can we check that out somehow?" I asked.

"If we could track down some of her friends and find a way to ask them about it," Phillip said, "then maybe."

"I have another idea," I said.

"I'd love to hear it."

"When we get back to April Springs after we touch base with Billy at the Claremont, let's go online and check out her social network pages. If there's one photo of her doing something more than three feet off the ground, we've caught her lying to us, and maybe we can use that against her."

After a moment or two of silence, Phillip said, "I hope you know how to do something like that, because honestly, I wouldn't have the first clue where to begin."

"No worries on that angle. Grace taught me," I said with a grin. "She's my tech guru."

"It must be nice to have one of those," Phillip said. "I'm not sure what we're going to tell George when we check in with him later."

"Don't be so hard on us! After all, we've made some real

progress," I said. "And who knows what Billy might have to tell us? One thing still troubles me, though."

"Just one? What's that?"

"We've eliminated all of our male suspects," I explained. "If one of the three women left on our list killed Cassandra, who exactly was she meeting at the Claremont, and is it even relevant to our investigation anymore?"

"When it comes to solving a murder, I don't believe there's such a thing as having *too* much information," Phillip said. "Let's at least see what Billy has to say."

"You're right. That sounds good to me," I said as I neared the inn. "Do you want to know something? I'm glad you were able to work on this investigation with me."

"So am I," he answered easily. "It feels good to be digging into something that happened within my lifetime again."

"Do you miss being the chief of police?" I asked him as I parked the Jeep.

"Only once in a while," he admitted. "Usually your mother keeps me so busy that I don't have much time to even think about it."

"She's one smart cookie, my momma," I said with a smile.

"I won't argue that point with you," he replied, adding a grin of his own. "We're both lucky to have her in our lives."

"Agreed," I said as we started up the walkway to the front door.

My hand was poised to open it when I heard someone calling me softly from the bushes off to one side. "Suzanne. Over here."

Billy was lurking in the shadows.

As Phillip and I joined him, I had to wonder why there was so much secrecy going on and just what the hotel clerk was about to tell us.

CHAPTER 14

"WHY ALL OF THE MYSTERY and intrigue?" I asked Billy as Phillip and I joined him in the shadows. From where he'd been standing, it appeared that he could keep an eye on the inside without anyone there seeing him.

"Did you see that woman with me earlier?" he asked.

"She appeared to be some kind of supervisor," I said.

"Actually, she's our regional personnel manager, and she's got a bug in her ear about me. I don't know why, but she's been hovering over me all day correcting my slightest mistake."

"Should you risk being out here talking to us, then? We don't want you jeopardizing your job for us," I said.

"We're fine. She should be gone for at least another half an hour. I checked on that receipt you showed me earlier. As a matter of fact, I was working the desk when Cassandra checked in."

"You knew her? Did she recognize you?"

"I don't think so. Now that I think about it, I'm pretty sure that she didn't," he said. "A lot of people just see the blazer, you know? You'd be amazed by how many people don't even make eye contact with lowly hotel clerks."

I knew the feeling, since some of my customers wouldn't make eye contact if I were on fire. "Billy, is there any chance you got a glimpse of who was meeting her here?"

"No, not while I was working the front desk," he said.

Phillip said, "But you saw someone later that you recognized."

"Yes," Billy admitted. "Twenty minutes after she checked in, I was taking one of our guests an extra room key when I spotted a guy I knew going into the room I'd assigned to Cassandra Lane."

"Who was it, Billy?"

"It was Darby Jones, a cop I know from April Springs."

"What? Are you absolutely sure about that?" I asked. What was Cassandra doing rendezvousing with one of April Springs's police officers while she was in a serious relationship with the mayor? That was just plain crazy, given the small size of our town. George was bound to find out, and sooner rather than later. Then I remembered Darby's reaction at the crime scene. I'd wondered at the time why he'd looked so shaken seeing the spot where Cassandra's lifeless body had been, and it could explain his cursory examination of her condo apartment. If they were seeing each other, he probably wouldn't be all that thrilled about going through her things.

Perhaps now I knew why.

"I started to say something to Darby, but he shook his head, warning me off," Billy said. "The truth is, I thought he was dating someone else, not the mayor's girlfriend."

"Did they look as though they were close?" Phillip asked.

"Well, most folks don't go to hotel rooms together that aren't, if you know what I mean," Billy said, shaking his head.

"What I mean is did you actually see the two of them together? Was there intimacy, or was something else going on?"

"That I couldn't say," Billy said. "All I know is that Darby was not very pleased that I spotted him sneaking into the lady's room. Not the ladies' room. Cassandra's room. Oh cripes!" That last bit was delivered as an expletive. I looked around, and coming up the walk was the woman we'd been discussing earlier, the one gunning for Billy. If she took three more steps, she'd spot him and have him dead to rights.

It was time for immediate action.

I met her while Billy scrambled back into the bushes, trying his best to duck out of sight. "Ma'am, I need to discuss something of vital importance with you."

I was counting on her training not to be rude to a guest, or in my case, a potential guest. "What can I do for you?"

"We need to talk," I said, steering her by grabbing her elbow and swinging her around so Billy could make his escape back into the building.

The woman was clearly not happy about me touching her. She resisted my tug, but it had served its purpose, as I saw Billy make his escape.

But what was I supposed to tell this woman now?

Phillip, bless his soul, took care of that for me. "We are here to commend that young man at the desk earlier. He quite possibly saved us a great deal of money by going above and beyond the call of duty identifying that dropped paper earlier in your lobby."

Wow. Not only had he explained our earlier presence, but he'd also managed to turn it around and make Billy look like a hero. "Is there someone of importance we can report his stellar actions to?"

"I'm in Personnel," she admitted.

"Well, I hope you know how lucky you are to have someone with such keen attention to detail. We will be holding our conference here next month all because of that conscientious young man, so I hope he'll be able to assist us personally when the time comes."

"Of course," she said. She may have had Billy in her sights before, but hopefully we'd managed to at least buy him a little time. What he did with it was entirely up to him. "May I ask the nature of your conference, and its size?"

Oh, no. She wasn't going to nail me down with any details about my imaginary convention. "We'll be in touch with the details later," I said as I put a hand on Phillip's arm. "We really must be going. We can't keep the president waiting."

What president that might have been was left entirely to the woman's imagination, but she seemed suitably impressed as we made our own escape.

"That was fast thinking on your part," I told Phillip as we got back into my Jeep.

"Me? You're the one who came up with some massive imaginary conference. Do you think it worked? Did we get Billy off the hook?"

"For now," I said, "but he's on his own now. What do you think of what he told us?"

"Officer Darby Jones is some kind of idiot," Phillip said without preamble. "We need to talk to that man pronto."

"You don't actually suspect him of murder, do you?" I asked as I headed back to April Springs.

"At this point I don't know what to think. All I do know for sure is that he's guilty of a lapse of judgment, at the very least."

We found Darby at his apartment, located along the road to Maple Hollow. It wasn't much of a place, and from the look of things through the front door, he hadn't done much in the way of making it homey. Darby was a big man, not fat but solid and stocky. He had a shock of thick black hair, and while I wouldn't have called him particularly handsome, he wasn't exactly homely, either. What had Cassandra seen in him worth jeopardizing her relationship with George, though? Maybe it was his youth and vitality, or maybe she was just the type of woman who couldn't stand being alone. Whatever the reason, Phillip and I needed to find out exactly what had happened between the young cop and the murder victim.

Darby looked surprised, and a bit unhappy, when he opened the door. "Hey you two. What's going on?" He glanced at Phillip. "Hey, Chief." Darby had been brought in after Phillip had retired, but I knew that there were some folks on the force who still called Jake Chief, though he'd only held the title a short time.

"Darby. We need to talk." There was no smiling or humor in Phillip's expression or his tone of voice.

Still, I was startled by the way Darby seemed to collapse in on himself. "I've been waiting for somebody to come by. Are you taking me in?"

"Why, did you kill Cassandra Lane?" Phillip asked him.

"No! But I've messed up, and bad. I figure I'm going to get fired. You know what? I probably deserve it." The man looked thoroughly beaten.

"May we come in and sit down?" I asked.

"I guess so," he said. It wasn't the warmest invitation I'd ever received, but then again, it was far from the coldest, too.

We made our way into the living room and sat on three mismatched chairs that all faced an older television sitting on a weathered wooden crate. Darby wasn't much for decorating, but then again, we weren't there for interior design tips.

Phillip took a deep breath, let part of it out slowly, and then he said solemnly, "Tell us all about it, son."

It was the "son" part that seemed to get to Darby. After a

few moments, he managed to compose himself enough to talk. "Does the mayor know?"

"We don't know," I said.

"You need to talk about what happened and get it off your chest," Phillip urged him. "It will do your spirit good."

Darby ran a hand through his thick hair and sighed. "I've got to do *something*. I've been waiting for someone to say something to me ever since I saw where she had been lying on the ground! I didn't go looking for her. It's important that you believe me."

"We believe you," I said. I wasn't sure if we did or not, but it was important to keep him talking, and if a little false reassurance was all that it took, I was more than willing to provide it.

"I was going through a bad breakup last week, and Cassandra saw me moping around on a bench under the town clock. She told me that she'd just come from seeing the mayor, and evidently she had problems of her own. We started talking, and I found myself pouring out my troubles to her. She told me that we were not all that different, and that we should help each other in our times of need. I didn't know what she meant; honest I didn't. I thought she just wanted to keep sharing sob stories, and I needed somebody to talk to. I thought it was a little odd when she invited me to the Claremont Inn in Union Square, but she told me that we couldn't meet in April Springs, and that she had the room there for a business meeting anyway, so I should come see her.

"The second I walked into that room, I knew that I'd made a bad mistake. She was wearing something flimsy, and there was a bottle of booze on the table, along with a pair of glasses. From the look of things, she'd managed to kill half of it before I'd even gotten there. I started to back out of the room the second I saw what was happening, but she managed to put her hand on the door so I couldn't get out without shoving her to one side, which I wasn't prepared to do. She tried to kiss me, but I told her I wasn't interested in her that way. I was just there to talk, and I told her so. Man, she got crazy upset when I said that! She screamed at me to get out, which I was more than happy to do, but once I was out the door, she kept chasing after me. I told her to get back inside, she wasn't dressed right, but she didn't care. Then she suddenly got really quiet, and a second after that, she started begging me to stay. She told me that there didn't have to be any strings. She just couldn't stand the thought of being alone. I'm ashamed to admit it, but I practically ran to my car and drove out of there as fast as I could. I felt bad about it, but not bad enough to go back.

"Anyway, I drove back to April Springs and went straight to bed. The next day I kept waiting for her to show up and say something, but I never saw her again. At least not alive. The next time I saw her was in front of your shop, with that donut on top of her. I nearly threw up when I saw her. You noticed something was off about me then, didn't you, Suzanne?"

"I thought something was going on, but I didn't know what," I admitted.

"My imagination was working overtime, and I figured you knew what was going on. I was so paranoid that I knew it was only a matter of hours before you showed up on my doorstep with the chief." He managed a soft grin. "I just thought it would be a different chief."

"You searched her place later, didn't you?" I asked him.

"When the chief told me to go over there, I just about died. I wasn't inside five minutes before I had to get out! I didn't kill her, but I just couldn't be there!" Darby took a deep breath, and then he turned to look at us both steadily for a moment before he spoke. "What are you two going to do about what I just told you? Are you going to tell the mayor? He'll kill me if he finds out. Worse yet, he'll probably get Chief Grant to fire me. I love this job, and I don't want to lose it."

"Well, *somebody* needs to tell the chief," Phillip said. "Don't you think that it would be better coming from you? I don't think you'll have to worry about losing your job, Darby. You didn't do anything wrong. Stupid, maybe, and more than a little naïve, but if you didn't kill her, you shouldn't have anything to worry about."

"Except the mayor's reaction when he hears the news about his girlfriend throwing herself at me," Darby said morosely.

"Do you want some advice?" I asked him.

"Sure. I'll do anything to get myself out of this jam."

"Tell George yourself before he hears it from someone else," I said simply.

Both men looked at me as though I'd lost my mind.

"Suzanne, that is a very bad idea," Phillip said.

"I agree with the chief," Darby echoed.

"Hear me out. The mayor might be a little gruff, but he's also a fair man. Let me put it this way. Would you rather he hear this from you, or from someone else who might not present it as fairly as you can?" I asked.

"The truth is that I'd rather he didn't know about it at all," Darby answered quickly.

"Let's pretend for a moment that's not an option," I said. "In a town the size of April Springs, we both know that's just wishful thinking, anyway."

"I'll tell him right after I tell the chief," he said, the defeat thick in his voice.

"I have an idea," I said, getting sudden inspiration. "Tell them both at the same time. That way if George does overreact, you've got the chief there to watch your back."

"Do you think he'll be enough if the mayor really wants to take a swing at me?" Darby asked.

It was a fair question. "I don't know, but at the very least, you only have to tell your story once instead of twice," I said.

"That makes sense," Phillip said. "She's right, son. It's best to get this over with, one way or the other."

Darby nodded. "I'll make the calls right now and get them together."

"Would you like us to stay?" I asked. I felt bad about making the police officer confess what had happened, even if he had played his own part in the debacle by not being aware of the situation he was getting himself into, innocently or not.

"Thanks anyway, but I've got to do this alone."

As we stood, Phillip put a hand on Darby's shoulder. "In an hour, this will all be over."

"That's what I'm afraid of," Darby said.

Once we were outside, Phillip said, "I can't believe Cassandra would throw herself at Darby like that. I never pegged her for that kind of behavior."

"I don't know if we can really be that hard on her," I said. "It sounds as though she knew that she was losing George, and despite it all, I think she truly loved him."

"Really? If that's the truth, she sure had an odd way of showing it," Phillip said as we neared my Jeep.

"She was in pain, so she acted rashly. I know Cassandra wasn't the easiest person in town to get along with, but she was human, just as frail and vulnerable as the rest of us."

"Do you honestly think of her as frail and vulnerable?" Phillip asked, the skepticism thick in his voice.

"Just because she put on a brave face most of the time doesn't mean that there wasn't a scared little girl down deep inside," I said. Somehow her behavior with Darby made me like her a little more, not because of her attempted betrayal of my friend, but because she had showed how flawed and unsure of herself she really was. I hadn't been all that fond of the brash and pushy woman, but at least I could relate to the pain she must have been feeling after being rejected by the man she loved and also the one she'd tried to seduce. It was odd finding myself feeling sympathy for Cassandra, but that was exactly how I felt. I'd never been desperate enough to do anything like that myself, but when I'd caught Max with Darlene, it had nearly broken me, so I could relate to the pain she must have been going through. I'd found solace in my family and friends, but Cassandra had neither one to fall back on. Clearly she'd done the only thing she knew how to do, which was to find comfort in someone else's arms, no matter how shallow and superficial it might have been.

"What now?" I asked Phillip as I got behind the wheel of the Jeep.

"Why don't we call it a night?" he asked. "I'm beat, and there's not much more we can do at the moment, anyway."

"That's true enough," I said. "Tomorrow after I close the donut shop for the day, we can talk to our primary suspects again."

"That sounds like a plan to me." As I drove him back to the donut shop where we'd left his truck, he asked me, "Suzanne, do you think there's the slightest chance that Darby might have killed her after all?"

The question shocked me a little. "No, I believe every word of what he told us. He had no reason to do it."

"I agree. That just leaves us with our final three suspects: Heather Lindquist, Marybeth Jenkins, and Mary Paris."

"It's hard to imagine one of those women climbing up on my roof with a pair of wire cutters, let alone committing murder," I said.

"Where did they even get the wire cutters, do you suppose?" Phillip asked.

"I've been wondering the same thing myself," I said as I pulled in beside his truck. "Let me make a call."

I got Francie right away. "Do me a favor. Check your toolbox for anything that's missing."

"I don't have to," Francie said, her voice leaden with despair. "I must have left my cutters on your roof. It's all my fault that woman was murdered!"

"Nonsense," I said, at least pleased that my hunch had turned out to be true.

"I don't see how it's *not* my fault," she said. "I told the police chief the second I noticed that they were missing. I was trimming off the ends of the wires, and they must have slipped out of my toolbox by accident when I tried to put them back in when I was up on the roof."

"There, you said it yourself. It was all an accident."

"Sorry, but I don't see it that way," she said. "If I hadn't left my cutters up there, then Cassandra wouldn't be dead right now."

"Francie, don't you think that if someone was determined to kill her, which they clearly were, they would have found another way?" The poor woman was clearly distraught about her tool being an accessory to murder.

"I guess so," she said.

"Then buck up," I replied as cheerfully as I could manage. "It wasn't your fault."

"I appreciate you saying it. I just wish I could believe you," she said.

CHAPTER 15

"**D**ID YOU GET ALL OF that?" I asked Phillip after I ended the call.

He nodded. "So, the killer took advantage of those cutters, which means that it probably wasn't premeditated after all. If that's the case, why was she up on the roof in the first place?"

"I don't know, but as soon as we catch her, we can ask her the same question," I said. "Are you ready to call it a night?"

"Yes, I'm talking to your mother in half an hour, and I want to be back home to make the call. Sorry Jake's away."

"It's fine," I said. "Don't forget, I was alone for a long time after Max left and before Jake and I got together."

"That's not exactly true though, is it? You still had your mother," Phillip said.

"That's true enough," I answered. "Get a good night's sleep, and I'll see you in the morning."

"See you at eleven," Phillip said. As he got out of the Jeep, he added, "Save me a few donuts tomorrow, would you? While the cat's away and all of that."

"Sure. What kind do you want?"

"You know me. Surprise me," he said with a grin, tapping my hood as he walked around to his truck. I thought about offering him the last dozen in the back of my Jeep, but I couldn't bring myself to do it. If he was going to consume the calories, I at least wanted them to be fresh. I'd chuck the donuts once I was back at the cottage.

After he was gone, I drove the short distance home, glancing over at Grace's darkened house as I passed it. I wondered how she was doing, and I thought about calling her, but I knew that if she wanted to talk, she knew where to find me.

After I walked in the door, I tossed the donuts, then I flipped on a few too many lights just to make it feel a little less lonely. I even turned on the television and put the Weather Channel on just to hear their voices. This was getting ridiculous. I was a grown woman, and yet I couldn't take a little bit of solitude. The way I saw it, I had three choices. I could go straight to bed, even though it was too early even for me, I could stay up another hour sitting in the cottage all alone, or I could go back out and be around other people, and not just on television.

I decided to go to the Boxcar and get some apple pie, if Trish had any left. After all, how could that *not* cheer me up? Instead of driving though, I decided to walk through the park. Not only was it closer that way, but it was a beautiful summer night. Things were finally starting to cool off a little in the evenings, and the humidity had been dropping a little bit every day. As I walked through the park, I passed several places that reminded me of my childhood, from the tree I'd fallen out of, breaking my arm in the process, to my secret place in the shadows where I used to love to hide from the world, to the place I'd first kissed Caleb Green. The park was like a map of my personal history, and what was more important, it felt like home to me as much as the cottage where I now lived with Jake. Above me, the stars were out in full force, at least what I could see of them through the canopy of leaves overhead, and by the time I got to the Boxcar Grill, I was already feeling better.

I didn't expect to run into the police chief leaving just as I was going up the steps.

"You're out late," Chief Grant said.

"What can I say? I'm turning into a night owl," I answered. "How goes the investigation?"

"I could ask you the same thing," he said with a tired grin. The man had really aged since he'd taken over the job, probably more spiritually than physically.

I decided to be completely candid with him, if for nothing else, as a complete change of pace. "Phillip and I have it narrowed down to three women."

The police chief was clearly taken aback by my unexpected candor. "To be honest with you, I wasn't expecting a straight answer. Let me see if I can figure out who you suspect. Heather Lindquist has to be there, and maybe Mary Paris, too?" he asked.

"I see we have the same lists. The only name you didn't mention was Marybeth Jenkins."

"That's because she's in the clear," he said with a nod.

"What? When did that happen?" That was certainly news to me.

"We found her in Hickory staying with her aunt. Can you believe it? She didn't even realize we were looking for her. Evidently she decided she needed to talk to someone older and wiser before she spoke with me."

"You said she was in the clear. What kind of alibi must she have had that you are willing to accept as true?" I asked. It was taking me a moment to get used to the fact that one of my main suspects had suddenly been stricken from my list. "She came right out and admitted to me that she had an argument with Cassandra right before she was killed."

"Not right before. We've got an eyewitness account that saw the last part of the argument. He said that when Marybeth drove away, Cassandra was actually laughing about the confrontation! After Marybeth drove off, he kept on walking his dog. It was a shame he didn't stick around. He might have been able to stop a murder."

"Who exactly *is* your witness?" I asked, curious as to who had seen the confrontation and why I was just hearing about it.

"I'm not going to tell you that," the chief said, scolding me a little as he added, "and you should know better than to even ask me. Take my word for it. Marybeth Jenkins didn't do it."

"Okay, I believe you. Have you learned anything else lately about Cassandra's last few days?" I asked as coyly as I could. Had Darby spoken with his boss and the mayor yet? It was the most delicate way that I could probe without coming right out and asking him myself.

The chief nodded. "You know perfectly well that I have. Darby told me that you were the one who convinced him to come clean with the mayor and me."

"How angry was George when he heard what happened?" I asked, being concerned about my friend. "Did he take a swing at Darby when he found out?"

"As a matter of fact, he just kind of melted right there in his chair. I'm guessing he suspected something was going on, and Darby just confirmed it. Poor old George looked absolutely lost. You might want to touch base with him when you get the chance. I've never seen a man so beaten down before in my life."

"I'll talk to him," I said, and then I asked a little hesitantly, "Did you fire Darby?" I needed to know, since I'd been the one who'd told him he had to share what had happened with him and Cassandra, no matter how bad it might make him look to his boss, and his boss's boss to boot.

"Why? For using poor judgment in his personal life? He didn't do anything illegal. I'm not happy with him, but that's no reason to fire the man."

"Good," I said. "Can you believe Cassandra threw herself at him like that?" I wasn't asking as idle gossip. I wanted to see if the chief had been as caught off guard as I had been by her behavior.

"Honestly, I've seen it before," he said. "When a powerful woman feels as though she's lost some of her mojo, she'll do just about anything to make sure that she still has whatever it was that put her on top. Cassandra was more vulnerable than a lot of people realized."

The insight surprised me. Apparently our police chief was growing up, and into his job, quite nicely. "Any word from Grace?" I asked him, almost afraid to bring her name up into our conversation.

"No, not really," he said flatly. "I called her, but she said it wasn't the time or the place to get into it, and I had to agree with her once I had a chance to think about it. We're going to talk more when she gets back, and that's all that I'm going to say on the subject."

"Understood," I said. I needed to get us back onto the topic of murder, anyway. "So, do you have any suspects besides the two I've named?"

Chief Grant looked around to make sure that we weren't being overheard. "I can't come right out and tell you that," he said as he shook his head. Was he scolding me again, or was it a clue that Phillip and I were in agreement with the police chief?

"So, you're saying that you can't say whether we're close to finding the killer or not," I asked. That was so cryptic I wasn't even sure that I understood what I'd been trying to say.

"We're following all of our leads, and we hope to make an arrest soon," he said, nodding.

What did that mean? "Seriously? You're getting *that* close? What do you know that we don't?"

The chief of police lowered his voice and stepped in closer to me. "Suzanne, I'm trying to tell you that we're both on the same page," he hissed, "but I'll deny it if you tell a soul I told you anything like that."

"I get it," I said softly in reply.

"Now I've got to get back to my desk. There are a few leads I still need to track down," he said as he started to walk away.

"Good luck," I called out, but he was already gone, striding off with real purpose as he headed back toward his office.

So, we'd all started out with a pretty strong list of suspects, and now we were down to the two finalists. One woman, Heather Lindquist, might have done it to revenge her brother's death in a skewed kind of way, while the other, Mary Paris, could have killed Cassandra for trying to assassinate her good name, which was certainly also within the realm of possibility. I had a feeling that I was missing something though, one final piece that would tell me who the actual killer was. But what was it? I stood there in the darkness outside of the Boxcar wracking my brain, but a direct assault was clearly not going to work. I had to back off and give my subconscious a chance to lead me to what I was missing.

In the meantime, I was going to have myself some pie.

Not only was I about to get some apple pie, but Trish's smile was a bonus as I walked into the Boxcar Grill.

"Suzanne, what are you doing here this late?" she asked with a smile.

"That's some warm greeting for a customer," I said, returning her grin. "The truth is, I felt like some apple pie and some company."

"You're in luck," she said with a grin. "I happen to have both. Sit right here and I'll be right back," she said as she ducked into the kitchen. Less than a minute later, she returned with two slices of apple pie adorned with hearty scoops of ice cream to boot. "Mind if I join you?"

"Do you mean those both aren't for me?" I asked as I laughed.

"If we get hungry after we eat these, I can always get more. There are some real perks to owning this place."

Trish put the plates on the table and sat beside me. I didn't even need the first bite to know that I was in for a treat. Good food, better yet good dessert, and a good friend were just what the doctor ordered for a bout of loneliness.

"How goes the case?" Trish asked me just as I was taking a bite of ice cream–laden pie.

After I finished it, I asked, "Did you purposely wait until I was eating to ask me that?"

"It's a skill I've acquired over the years," she said with a grin. "Haven't you noticed that most servers don't check on how you like your meal until you've got a full bite in your mouth?"

"I always just thought that was a coincidence," I said.

She grinned at me. "No, it's how we like to mess with you. You never answered me, though. How is it going? I wasn't Cassandra's biggest fan, but being squashed by a giant donut is not a fate I'd wish on anyone."

"Me, either," I said, flashing back to the image that I was afraid would be permanently burned into my mind. We were the only two people in the diner. "Are you even supposed to be open right now?" I asked her.

"No, I flipped the CLOSED sign the second you walked in," she said happily.

"So I'm keeping you here past your regular business hours," I replied, feeling a little guilty about it.

"Suzanne, I wanted to spend a little time with you," she said firmly. "You aren't *making* me do a thing that I don't want to do. So talk. Who do we suspect?"

156

I suddenly realized that there wouldn't be any harm in sharing our findings with Trish. Besides, it might help me to clarify my own thoughts by expressing what I knew to someone not so closely associated with the case. "Okay, but remember, you asked for it. First off, there's a woman named Heather Lindquist involved. As a matter of fact, she was in here earlier. You've got to remember her storming out."

"I remember. What's she got to do with the case?"

"Cassandra got her brother's killer off from the murder charge, and Heather threatened to get revenge for what she'd done."

Trish shuddered a little. "That's a pretty powerful motive."

"I know. The other suspect left on our list is a lot closer to home. Phillip and I think Mary Paris might be involved." It sounded odd coming out of my own mouth, but the facts couldn't be ignored. Mary might not have had as much motivation as Heather did, but if her cleaning service was all she had, she couldn't afford to lose her sterling reputation. If folks believed Cassandra's story, they might not use Mary the next time, and I knew better than most how quickly bad news, especially gossip, traveled in a small town.

"Mary?" Trish asked, puzzled by the reference. "Hasn't she had enough problems lately without you accusing her of murder?"

"What do you mean?" I asked after taking my last bite of pie and ice cream. It had been so delicious that I thought about asking for another piece, but if I did that, I probably wouldn't be able to fit into my jeans in the morning.

"She's just gone through a bad breakup, and now you suspect her of killing Cassandra," Trish said as she stood and cleared our plates away.

That was right! I'd heard George mention the same thing, but I hadn't put much significance to it.

That's when I realized that might be the missing piece after all! "Was she dating Darby Jones, by any chance?" I asked Trish.

"Yes, of course. I thought you knew about it."

"As a matter of fact, I didn't, and I'm willing to bet that the chief didn't know, either," I said as I stood up quickly. "Sorry to eat and run, but I have to go."

"Why the rush?" Trish asked me as I tried to hand her a ten-dollar bill, which she was quite adept at refusing. "By the way, that was two friends sharing dessert, not something I'm going to bill you for."

"Thanks," I said, not even fighting her on it. I grabbed my cell phone as I hurried out of the diner. I had to tell the police chief what I'd just managed to put together. It still wasn't enough to condemn Mary Paris for murder, but it was certainly a way he could use to try to crack her. Her motive for murder, which had been borderline before, suddenly became pretty strong, especially if she'd heard that Cassandra had thrown herself at her recently former boyfriend.

My call to Chief Grant went straight to voicemail, and I was about to leave a message when I heard footsteps in the gravel behind me.

"Put the phone down, Suzanne," an icy voice said as the woman I'd just been discussing with Trish stepped out of the shadows and into the light from the nearby streetlamp.

It was Mary Paris, and in her hand was one of the biggest, sharpest knives I'd ever seen in my life, now pointing straight at my heart!

CHAPTER 16

"I WAS AFRAID YOU MIGHT BE too clever for your own good," Mary said as she gestured to my cell phone. "Throw that thing into the weeds, if you don't mind." When I hesitated, she made a slight stabbing motion with the knife. "Suzanne, I'm not afraid to use this. After all, they can't very well execute me twice if I commit another murder."

I thought about throwing my phone at her and running, but I knew that would be taking my own life into my hands. The prospect of having that knife jammed into my back as I fled was enough to panic me a little, waiting for it to plunge into my flesh. I did as I was told, though I wasn't about to go down without a fight. I just had to come up with a better plan than running away and hoping for the best. "Mary, what are you talking about?" I asked her, trying to play it as innocently as I could. "What's going on?"

"Drop the act," she said heatedly. "You know I did it. I was wondering when you'd put it all together. What finally gave me away?" the killer asked.

Maybe if we stood there long enough, Trish would come out, or perhaps a late customer hoping for a bite after hours might come instead. If I could get some reinforcements, I might just make it out of this confrontation alive. "I don't know what you're talking about," I said as I glanced at the road and then at the donut shop across the street. Where *was* everybody? Then again, I realized that there was little call for traffic on that particular part of the road at night. Jake was gone, and so was Grace, so that was the sum total of residents besides me beyond Gabby's shop and my donuts. Still, someone had to be out!

Mary must have realized it herself. "Let's take a little walk, shall we?" She gestured with the knife into the woods of the park. I'd fled a killer there once before, and only luck had saved me that time. Could I count on it again, or was this going to be my last case, as well as my final breath?

I didn't have much choice.

I did as she asked, though there hadn't been much of a request to her demand. "Why kill her, Mary? Was it about the pin, or was it about Darby?"

"*I* knew I hadn't taken that pin, so I figured it would turn up and I'd be vindicated. It was the way she threw herself at my boyfriend that killed Cassandra."

"He wasn't your boyfriend anymore though, was he?" I asked.

We were getting away from the lights of the Boxcar, and we weren't yet to the next set of lights deeper into the park. Just up ahead and off to one side was the hiding spot I'd found as a child that was safe from all of the lights, a narrow opening in a thick copse of trees, but I hadn't hidden there for years. Was any of it still there in the darkness? I'd had my own little spot in the shadows, and I remembered using an old discarded metal fencepost as a sword long ago. Surely it had been discovered by some other curious child since then, but was there a chance my salvation lay there? I started steering Mary toward the entrance, hoping that she didn't notice that I was now going in a purposeful direction and not taking some random walk.

"He belonged to *me*," she snarled, and the knife flicked forward suddenly.

I felt the breeze of it on my elbow as it came within a hair's breadth of cutting me. As dangerous as goading her was, I couldn't afford to stop. The only chance I had was to get her angry enough to lose her focus long enough for me to get something to fight back with.

"How did you even know Cassandra was interested in him?"

"I followed him to the Claremont Inn," she said icily. "I'd been trailing him for a few days, just after I saw him having a deep conversation with Cassandra in the middle of town. When she opened that hotel room door in her lingerie, I knew that I had to end her!"

"You didn't stay long after that, did you?" I asked her, taking another step toward what I hoped was my salvation, a last chance at saving my own life.

"No, there was nothing left that I needed to see," she said.

"It's a shame you didn't hang around. If you had, Cassandra might still be alive."

"What are you talking about, Suzanne?" She looked clearly puzzled by my statement.

I was getting closer to the opening now, but I still couldn't make out the entrance to my little safe haven. It had to still be there though, and I'd know it when I got close enough to the entrance.

"Darby rejected her as soon as he figured out what was going on," I said. "She ran after him, chased him out of her room trying to get him to come back, but he wouldn't do it."

"He still *loves* me?" Mary asked, her voice cracking with hope.

I hadn't said anything to make her assume that, but sure, why not use it? "He probably did, but do you honestly think he's going to want you now that you're a cold-blooded killer? Why did you push that donut on her, anyway? You couldn't have planned it."

"I was on the roof spying on her," she admitted. "I just knew she was meeting Darby, and I had to see it for myself. When no one showed up though, she was about to leave. I'd spotted the wire cutters on the roof, so I decided to take care of her once and for all. It was easy and remarkably quiet to snip those wires, and when she got right under the donut, I gave it a good hard push!"

I was nearly there! I could even see the faint outline of the break in the trees. Two more steps and I'd be there! I had to stretch this out for just another few moments. "It was you that Marybeth nearly ran down in her car, wasn't it?" I asked.

"What? No, of course not. I never saw her that night," she said. "Whatever gave you that idea?"

Okay, it was impossible for anyone to be right all of the time. Still, my question had served its purpose. I finally saw the break in the trees, and without an ounce of hesitation, I dove into the opening. If someone had found my spot and taken that fencepost out, I was a goner.

There was no place to run from there.

And then my heart sank.

When I reached down for the fencepost, I realized that it was gone.

Maybe I should have made a run for it after all.

It appeared that my time had finally run out.

I couldn't just stand there and let Mary stab me to death, though. I got down on all fours, searching for anything I might use to fight back, as Mary broke into the opening and stood over me. There was just enough light for me to see what was happening, mostly because my eyes had adjusted to the low level of light that was coming from the park.

As I scrambled on my hands and knees, searching for anything I might use in my own defense, I felt something.

It was the post, still there after all of these years, waiting for me in my time of need.

With a blood-curdling scream, Mary brought the knife down toward my face, ready to bury it to its hilt.

Pulling the post free from a few weeds trapping it to the ground, I found some kind of superhuman strength and held it above my head.

I didn't block the blow, but I managed to deflect it to one side.

The knife sliced my shirt on the way down, and then it was buried in the dirt.

Now *I* had the upper hand.

But not for long.

CHAPTER 17

I TRIED TO USE THE THIN metal post to strike out at Mary, but she somehow managed to grab it as I swung it toward her, deflecting my blow as well. Her hands found purchase on the steel just above mine, and as we wrestled for control, I felt my grip slowly slipping away. This woman was either stronger than I was, more than a little bit insane, or perhaps even some of both.

I had one last option, or I knew that I was a dead woman.

I suddenly released the post, and Mary flew backward from the sudden lack of any resistance on my part. She fell through the opening, and as she did, I scrambled to retrieve the knife, still buried in the ground beside me. Could I honestly stab her if she came back at me? In ordinary circumstances I doubted that I could bring myself to do it, but these weren't ordinary circumstances. If I didn't kill her, she would surely murder me, and when it came down to it, I wanted to live.

I just hoped that my strength, and my willpower, were stronger than hers.

After a few moments that felt like lifetimes though, I began to wonder what was going on.

She didn't come back in after me.

Lying low to the ground, I crawled out of the opening, ready to fight her off if she was waiting to strike out at me.

Instead, I saw her running away in the faint light, back toward the road.

There was only one thing I could do.

I chased after her, the knife weaving and bobbing as I ran.

Mary must have seen me as she looked back over her shoulder, still on the run. The woman looked absolutely terrified to be facing the knife she'd recently tried to use on me.

And that was her downfall.

She must have forgotten how close she was to the road.

As Mary Paris put her foot on the pavement, a car, a police squad car actually, came out of the darkness and hit her full on, sending Mary, still gripping the fencepost in one hand, flying through the air.

CHAPTER 18

"**I**S SHE DEAD?" I ASKED as I leaned over her crumpled body.

The police chief didn't have time to answer me; he was busy searching for a pulse. Chief Grant was white and shaking, but he was still doing his best to keep it together. "I never saw her until the last second. She came out of nowhere."

"Mary was trying to kill me," I told him breathlessly.

"I've got something. It's weak, but at least it's there," the chief said, the relief strong in his voice. He called for an ambulance, and as we waited for it to show up, we both sat in the road by Mary's side in the light of his headlights. She muttered a few things and tried to move, but she never said anything that I could understand.

Once the EMTs got there, they made quick work of bundling her up on their gurney and carting her off.

"I need to go to the hospital to see how she is," the chief said, still visibly shaking from what had just happened.

"Pull your cruiser over in front of my donut shop," I said. "I'll get my Jeep and drive us."

"You don't have to do that," he said, his voice starting to crack a little as he said it.

"Wait right here for me. I mean it," I said. I ran, not through the park, but down the road, collected my Jeep, and held my breath as I raced back to pick the police chief up.

To my relief, he was still there, standing beside his parked cruiser and looking more like a zombie than the chief of police.

"What happened, Suzanne?" he asked me as I drove us to the hospital. "Why was she trying to kill you?"

"Mary was dating Darby before they broke up," I said. "When she found out about Cassandra's play for him, she lost her mind. It was really never about the pin."

"I didn't even know they'd been dating, and he was on my force," the chief said.

"You can't know *everything* that happens around here," I said, doing my best to console him.

"Maybe not, but I should have at least known *that*. Darby tried to share his personal problems with me last week, but I was too busy to listen. Maybe Grace was right. Maybe this job has changed me so much that I'm not that nice a guy anymore."

"You don't have to worry about that. He's still in there," I said, patting his chest. "You just need to let him come out every now and then."

"Maybe," the chief said.

Once we were at the hospital, he seemed better, and when a few of his officers came in, including Darby, I knew that he was in good hands.

There was nothing left for me to do there, so I headed back home.

I wasn't sure if I'd even be able to catch a little sleep before I had to open the donut shop, but I was going to at least try.

CHAPTER 19

I T WAS BRUTAL GETTING UP for work the next morning. I couldn't have gotten more than four hours of sleep, and I knew that there was going to be a long nap in my future once I closed the place down for the day. Not only that, but I still had a party to plan. After all, I was still in desperate need of an influx of cash, and the anniversary festivities were the only way I was going to get my hands on any. I was sure that I'd be having a long chat with the police chief about what had happened with Mary. I called the hospital and found out that she was in stable but guarded condition, whatever that meant. Whatever the outcome, her fate was not in my hands, and I didn't regret a thing I'd done that might have contributed to her situation at the moment. After all, she'd been trying to kill me, and I'd fought back to save my own life.

The consequences were hers to bear.

I was getting ready to take my break after finishing the cake donuts and starting on the dough for the yeast ones when I remembered the lottery tickets in my wallet. I nearly threw them away without even scratching off the numbers, but I just couldn't bring myself to do it. Taking the ticket Phillip had given me, recognizable by the dog-eared corner, I scratched the numbers to find no prize revealed, just as I'd expected.

The second one was a different story altogether, though.

After scratching the numbers and seeing that I had a match, I started to remove the coating over the prize I'd won. Most likely it was a free ticket, or maybe two dollars, a slim victory and not enough to do me much good.

I had to stare at the revealed number on the ticket a full minute before it finally sank in.

I hadn't won the main prize of one hundred thousand dollars, but it was still amazing when I discovered that I'd won a lesser prize, if you could call it that, of ten thousand dollars. It wasn't enough to retire on by any means, and I knew that taxes would take a big bite out of it before I saw a dime, but it should still be enough to cover nearly all of my donut shop's losses over the past few months! Technically, I supposed we didn't have to have the party after all, but I was going forward with it full steam ahead. Before, it had been a last-ditch effort to save my donut shop, but now, it could honestly be what I'd be telling the world what it really was, a celebration commemorating a decision that had changed the course of my life forever.

I decided to try to get Jake on the phone. If I woke him, I had a hunch that he'd forgive me.

To my delight, he answered right away, though he was whispering as he did.

"Hey, Suzanne."

"Hi, Jake. I can't believe that you're actually awake."

"Truth be told I was just heading off to bed. I was just thinking about calling you. Great minds think alike, don't they? How is your day going so far?"

"Better than most, but I miss you," I said. I was going to tell him about our lottery win, but for a moment, I just wanted to relish the sound of his voice. Our win wasn't exactly life-changing money, but it was coming at a time when I could really use it.

But more than the cash, more than all of the money in the world, I knew that I was richer than most in what really counted, and that was having a husband I loved and who luckily loved me back just as much.

"Ready for some good news for a change of pace?" I asked him with a grin spread on my face as I prepared myself to share our good fortune.

RECIPES

Apple Cinnamon Donuts

From time to time, my family and I get on a health kick, if you can call eating donuts being healthy. The truth is, I've acquired a taste for baked donuts over the years, and these are some of my favorites. One member of my family enjoys these better than the fried ones, or so they tell me. If you've never baked a donut before, be prepared for something more cake-like in preparation, taste, and texture, but hey, how can anyone think that being close to cake is a bad thing? I've heard that some folks like to make their icing for these with a hint of apple juice or cider when combined with confectioner's sugar instead of the usual water or milk, though I know for a fact that those things work beautifully, too. Warmed apple butter is another variation we occasionally use to smear across the top of fresh donuts, but remember, *any* way you top them, they are delicious.

Ingredients

- 2 packets dry yeast
- 1/2 cup warm water
- 1/2 cup granulated sugar
- 1 1/2 cups applesauce
- 3 tablespoons butter or margarine, melted
- 2 teaspoons cinnamon

- 1 teaspoon nutmeg
- 1/2 teaspoon salt
- 2 eggs, lightly beaten
- 5 1/2 to 6 1/2 cups all-purpose flour

Topping
- 1/2 cup butter, melted
- 1/2 cup sugar
- 1 tablespoon cinnamon

Directions

Dissolve the yeast in the warm water in a large bowl, allowing it to sit 5 to 10 minutes.

I use my stand mixer bowl for this step. In the same bowl, to the dissolved yeast add the sugar, applesauce, melted butter, cinnamon, nutmeg, salt, beaten eggs, and 3 cups of the flour. Beat this at low speed with an electric mixer for 2 minutes, or by hand, until the mixture is moistened throughout, then beat at medium speed for another minute.

Stir in 2 1/2 cups of flour, one half cup at a time, adding it until you've formed a soft dough. The consistency of the dough is more important than the exact amount of flour you use. Turn it out onto a lightly floured surface, and knead it about 5 minutes, or until it's smooth and elastic.

Place the dough in a bowl coated with cooking spray, then lightly spray the top of the dough. Cover it with a clean cloth and let it rise in a warm place free from drafts for about an hour. It should have almost doubled in size by then. Punch the dough down, and then turn it out onto a lightly floured surface.

Roll the dough to 1/2-inch thickness, and then cut it with your donut cutter. Place the donuts and holes on greased baking sheets, then brush the tops of donuts with some of the melted butter. Let the donuts rise, uncovered, in a warm, draft-free place for 30 minutes. Bake the donuts at 425°F for 11 minutes or until they are golden. Immediately brush melted butter over baked donuts as soon as you take them out, and then dip the donuts into the sugar-cinnamon mix.

Makes 12 to 16 donuts.

The Best Apple Pie I've Ever Made, or Eaten, for That Matter

Over the years, whenever family gets together, whenever there's a birthday, or when we have any other cause for celebration, there is usually a request for my apple pie. With a crumb topping and a blend of Granny Smith and Gala apples, it is simply out of this world.

I used to make homemade crust just as my dear sweet late mother-in-law taught me, including the liberal use of lard in the mix, but now I grab a shell from the freezer section. After all, the apples are the star of this show, just as it should be!

Ingredients

- 8 – or 9-inch pie crust, premade

Filling
- 1/2 cup granulated sugar
- 3 tablespoons flour
- 1/2 teaspoon nutmeg
- 1/2 teaspoon cinnamon
- Dash of salt
- 5–6 cups thinly sliced firm, tart apples (Granny Smiths work well, with a nice blend of Gala to taste)

Topping
- 1 cup flour
- 1/2 cup brown sugar
- 1/2 cup butter, room temperature

Directions

Preheat your oven, peel and core the apples, then cut them into thin slices. I used to do this by hand, but I've got a gadget now that does all that for me, and besides, it's fun to use as the apples make their journey through the machine, spiraling out the peel as I go. We've started leaving these peels out for the squirrels and rabbits in the yard, which they absolutely adore!

In a regular-sized bowl, sift together the sugar, flour, nutmeg, cinnamon, and salt, then stir this mixture into the apples until they are thoroughly coated. Add the coated apples to the shell, and then, taking another bowl, combine the flour and brown sugar, then cut in the butter. The mix should be crumbly and the butter still in small pea-sized chunks. Add these to the top, then bake the entire pie uncovered in a 425°F oven for 30 to 45 minutes, until the crust is golden brown and a butter knife slips into the top easily. For the last 15 or so minutes of baking, I like to loosely tent aluminum foil over the top to allow the apples to bake further. You should see a little juice bubbling around the edges when the pie is finished.

Apple Cider Donuts

This is one of my favorite holiday donut recipes. They are quite good any time of year, but I love to make these when the leaves begin to change their hues, and I continue making them up until Christmas. The first step of heating the cider is one of my favorite things to do in any recipe (besides sampling the results, of course), sending delicious aromas through the air. Happy thoughts and warm memories of those I love embrace me as I make these donuts, and that alone is worth the effort it takes to make them.

Ingredients

- 3/4 cup apple cider
- 1 cup granulated sugar
- 1/4 cup margarine, soft
- 2 eggs
- 1/2 cup buttermilk
- 4 cups all-purpose flour
- 2 teaspoons baking powder
- 1 teaspoon baking soda
- 1 teaspoon nutmeg
- 1 teaspoon cinnamon
- 1/2 teaspoon salt
- canola oil, enough to cover and fry the donuts

Directions

Heat the apple cider to its boiling point in a shallow saucepan for 10 minutes, then remove the pan from the heat completely and let it cool. In the meantime, cream the butter and sugar together in a large bowl until the mixture is smooth. Beat the eggs, add the buttermilk, and then add this to the mix, stirring thoroughly as you go. Next, sift together the flour, baking powder, baking soda, nutmeg, cinnamon, and salt. Add the dry ingredients to the wet, stirring just enough to blend them all together. Place the dough on a floured surface and roll out until it's between 1/2 and 1/4 inch thick. Cut out donut shapes or diamonds, or use your donut cutter to make round solid shapes if you prefer.

Fry the donuts in canola oil at 370°F until brown, flipping halfway through the process. This will take 3 to 5 minutes. Drain on paper towels, then dust them with powdered sugar.

Makes approximately 2 dozen donuts.

Delightful Homemade Fried Apple Pies

Sometimes I get lazy, even when it comes to making donuts, as well as other treats for me and my family, and I'm sure that if you've cooked or baked long enough for yours, there are times when you feel the same way I do. When I want my loved ones to have something special and homemade but I don't want to spend hours making it, this is one of the recipes I turn to. The results are unbelievable, and I get more raves for this treat than I do from some of my offerings that take a great deal more time and effort to make!

Ingredients

- Precooked apple pie filling, 8 oz., from the can (cherry or any other pie filling works too)
- 1 tablespoon sugar
- 1 teaspoon cinnamon
- 1 ready-made pie crust
- canola oil, enough to cover and fry the apple pies

Directions

While the canola oil is heating, I always like to start this recipe by warming the apple pie filling on the stovetop over low heat, adding the sugar and cinnamon and mixing it well, then taking the pan off the heat to cool a little.

Next, I unroll the pie crust onto the countertop. You can make your own crust if you'd like, but remember, this is quick and simple, and there are times I seem to have an extra crust in the freezer just waiting for me to make these treats.

Flour the rim of a drinking glass and cut circles out of the defrosted but still chilled dough by pressing down and twisting.

I am usually able to get four circles out of one crust, but that will all depend on the size glass you choose.

Next, I place a small amount of cooled apple pie filling in the center of each circle, then wet the edges of the dough all the way around with water. Folding the dough over in half, I pinch the edges together, sealing in the filling. The shape will look something like a curved half moon.

Next, I carefully drop the pies into 375°F oil and give them 3 to 4 minutes on each side before turning them with skewers. The crusts will puff out a little along the edges, and they will get golden, with maybe a little brown as well. These usually take about 8 minutes altogether to cook, but the time can vary. Don't be afraid to leave them in a little longer than you would normally fry something.

Lastly, pull the pies from the oil, dust them with powdered sugar, and they're ready to eat.

Makes 4 pies.

If you enjoy Jessica Beck Mysteries and you would like to be notified when the next book is being released, please visit our website at jessicabeckmysteries.net for valuable information about Jessica's books, and sign up for her new-releases-only mail blast.

Your email address will not be shared, sold, bartered, traded, broadcast, or disclosed in any way. There will be no spam from us, just a friendly reminder when the latest book is being released, and of course, you can drop out at any time.

OTHER BOOKS BY JESSICA BECK

The Donut Mysteries
Glazed Murder
Fatally Frosted
Sinister Sprinkles
Evil Éclairs
Tragic Toppings
Killer Crullers
Drop Dead Chocolate
Powdered Peril
Illegally Iced
Deadly Donuts
Assault and Batter
Sweet Suspects
Deep Fried Homicide
Custard Crime
Lemon Larceny
Bad Bites
Old Fashioned Crooks
Dangerous Dough
Troubled Treats
Sugar Coated Sins
Criminal Crumbs
Vanilla Vices
Raspberry Revenge
Fugitive Filling
Devil's Food Defense
Pumpkin Pleas
Floured Felonies
Mixed Malice
Tasty Trials
Baked Books
Cranberry Crimes
Boston Cream Bribes
Cherry Filled Charges
Scary Sweets
Cocoa Crush
Pastry Penalties
Apple Stuffed Alibies

The Classic Diner Mysteries
A Chili Death

A Deadly Beef
A Killer Cake
A Baked Ham
A Bad Egg
A Real Pickle
A Burned Biscuit

The Ghost Cat Cozy Mysteries
Ghost Cat: Midnight Paws
Ghost Cat 2: Bid for Midnight

The Cast Iron Cooking Mysteries
Cast Iron Will
Cast Iron Conviction
Cast Iron Alibi
Cast Iron Motive
Cast Iron Suspicion